Get a Grant: Yes You Can!

by Dennis M. Norris

SCHOLASTIC
PROFESSIONAL BOOKS

New York * Toronto * London * Auckland * Sydney

To my all-time favorite teacher . . .
Cordelia Zinkan
Fifth Grade, Charles Elementary School
Richmond, Indiana
1969–70

Teachers may photocopy the designated reproducible pages for classroom use. No other part of this publication may be reproduced in whole or in part, or stored in a retrieval system, or transmitted in any form or by any means, electronic, mechanical, photocopying or otherwise, without written permission of the publisher. For information regarding permission, write to Scholastic Inc., 555 Broadway, New York, NY 10012.

Cover design by Vincent Ceci

Interior illustrations by Teresa Anderko

Interior design by Ellen Matlach Hassell
for Boultinghouse & Boultinghouse, Inc.

ISBN 0-590-96387-2

Copyright © 1998 by Dennis M. Norris. All rights reserved.

Printed in the USA.

Contents

An Overview

The most wonderful thing about trying for a grant is that the process never ends. You begin with an idea and develop it into a workable project. As you implement the project, you come up with more ideas, or better approaches to the idea you already have in place. A grant to fund your ideas means official recognition of your creative approach to an education problem. You will find that your creativity and success breed more of the same, and that other funders will step in to offer supplementary support for the grant that you've already received. Isn't it a fantastic world!

The Grant Bug

A grant can bring real fulfillment to you as a professional. You will find that your organization and success will intrigue other teachers. They will want to know how you've accomplished this wonderful result. Other funders will also be intrigued, chipping in additional funding here and there to keep you on the road to success. Feel proud of yourself. You deserve all of this attention!

Once you have built a creative and effective grant team, and once your first grant has come and gone, you will be bitten by the grant bug forever. Remember to stay organized and focused on obtaining grants. Allow yourself to take a deep breath and relax once in awhile. There are enough grants out there for everyone. The next one you go after should be as carefully researched and analyzed by the grant team as was the first one.

While it is not a requirement that your school be involved with only one grant project at a time, that is certainly an idea to carefully consider. Some grants become time consuming for everyone involved in the project. If you have the resources to go after more grants, then I say more power to you! However, biting off more than you can chew can be disastrous, and it will show in your performance no matter how organized you are. Not only will funders balk at funding you in the future, but you will probably have to do some quick talking to get your collaborators back in line. Avoid all this with careful planning and open communications within your team. Make each grant the best it can be and it will benefit you in the long run. This book will lead you through the entire grant process and empower you to view the field of grants as fertile ground on which your creative ideas may play out. Millions of dollars are available in the form of education grants, so let's get going.

Chapter 1

Grants Fund Ideas

The majority of grants fund *ideas*, not *needs*. It is rare to receive a grant based solely on a need. Funders are more than willing to fund your needs if you have a wonderfully creative idea at the core of your project. Of course, it's tempting to think of a grant as a way to pay for immediate needs in a school. After all, your school can probably use additional technology, updated playground equipment, or an outdoor education center.

NEED	IDEA
additional technology	literacy project
updated playground equipment	physical fitness program
outdoor education center	study of native wildlife

Grants must also address problems or issues in education. Here again, the funder isn't concerned with needs. Government agencies and other public/private funders are interested in general areas such as intergenerational illiteracy, violence in schools, access to the Internet, or children's self-esteem. Your creative ideas for grants must address a problem and must offer your effective solution. You and your funder then agree on what the problem is, that your proposed solution is reasonable and within the funder's guidelines, and that your solution is creative.

Project CROAK! Takes Off

Project CROAK! (Creeks, Rivers, Oceans and Kids!) is the best example I can give showing the power of ideas. The third-grade team at one of our elementary schools called me and wanted a grant to obtain site licensing for a popular software program. The team was thinking in terms of *needs* and was having trouble identifying what educational problems the grant would address. "Look at yourselves, at your grade level, your building, surroundings, school district, and community." I said. I asked them to do a self-evaluation that answered "Who are we?" and "What makes us special?"

The teachers were proud that their school emphasized study in natural and environmental science. Several parents and professional organizations connected to the school provided field trip opportunities, special resources, and guest speakers—all in an effort to integrate environment studies into every part of the curriculum. For example, every fall, the third-graders raise tad-

> Creativity drives my decision-making as a teacher and technology coordinator. But I always have some piece of equipment in mind as I think of creative projects. That's what makes the ideas real.
>
> *Jackie Carrigan, Technology Coordinator, Plainfield Community Schools, Plainfield, Indiana*

poles in their classroom. When the tadpoles become frogs they are released into a creek that runs behind the school.

I asked the teachers to brainstorm grant ideas, keeping in mind that grants address problems or issues in education. They identified three separate issues.

Issue 1 Students were aware of concepts like pollution and ecology, but were not sensitive to the interdependence of environmental systems and the importance of working with others to keep the environment healthy.

Issue 2 Students were not expected to be skilled in using computers. They needed to improve their computer skills.

Issue 3 Technology skills were often taught only with science or mathematics. The teachers sought a grant project that would result in children who were environmentally-sensitive, technology literate, and creative enough to apply technology in many different ways.

We had come a long way from the simple, original need for software, but we still needed a wildly creative idea.

Time for Innovation

An idea occurred to me: Why not come up with a fictitious story in which we could include the *real* event of releasing frogs into the creek? The entire project would be based on the premise that certain conditions along the waterway might harm or help the frog as it made its way downstream. In our story, one of the frogs would escape and make its way down a series of creeks and rivers that eventually led to the Mississippi River, then out to the Gulf of Mexico. Partner schools in various towns would be along the route. At the start of every month our school would send to partner schools a disk holding a mug shot of our missing frog, environmental information on our portion of the waterway, and a geographical profile of our area. We would ask "Have you seen our frog?" Using similar software, partner schools would then produce their own disks about their portion of the waterway. The result would be a comprehensive CD-ROM that covered the entire waterway, its geography, and its pollution problems.

Children doing this project would learn cause and effect: Throwing a soda can into the water, for example, could lead to pollution along the waterway's entire length. The most interesting part of the project allowed each partner school to create and publish a story about how the frog got from one point to another during its travels. So not only would the children learn scientific facts while using their computers, they would also use them for creative writing.

See Project CROAK! Leap

The *need* of the third-grade teachers in this project became peripheral to the wonderful *idea* about a runaway frog. Project CROAK! initially received small $100 to $500 grants from local supporters and the school district's education foundation. Yet these small grants sparked an interest that, in a few months, led to major funding from the National Environmental Education & Training Foundation, Chevron U.S.A., and GTE. One year later it was named by the Council of Great Lakes States Governors as one of the top technology projects of 1995. As of the writing of this book, it is being developed into a national environmental project that will involve more than one hundred different watersheds in the United States and Canada. As with many successful grant projects, Project CROAK! was first based on need, followed by self-assessment, the identification of an educational problem or issue, brainstorming, creativity, and, finally, success.

Brainstorming and Creativity Count

I can't stress enough how important brainstorming and creativity are to grant writing. Teachers must be willing to be innovate, to push the envelope, to step outside the boundaries at every opportunity. That won't be hard. I've always been impressed by the ability of teachers to find ways of getting what they need for their students.

Creativity means developing confidence and trust in yourself and your colleagues. You must buy into your ideas yourself before you can sell them to someone else. The enthusiasm and excitement you feel for your project will

How Did You Think of That?

Here are two case histories that illustrate creative ideas that could lead to a grant.

Case History 1: A group of teachers thought of a creative way to get their kids to read. They partnered with four other classrooms around their city. The teachers went to the airport and spoke with an airline offering international flights. The pilots and flight attendants agreed to bring back flags, currency, menus, and other items from specific countries and cultures throughout the school year. Meanwhile, the classes read stories in which they found numeric clues that helped them figure out the latitude and longitude of one of the airline's client countries. The kids then studied the different countries and cultures. At the end of the school year, the airline employees joined the kids for a reading and multicultural fair.

Case History 2: An elementary school teacher wanted her kids to become more widely aware and appreciative of the world. To do this, she used astronomy and geography. She divided her class into several groups; each group mapped a constellation the children had identified in the night sky. After identifying each of the stars in the constellation, the kids drew a proportional replica of the constellation over a map of the United States. They then looked for schools in towns that were located within constellation patterns, schools they could e-mail. Kids from across the country used e-mail to talk about their towns, schools, communities, and which constellations could be seen from their location.

flow naturally onto the written page. Look at it this way: Funding agencies employ people to read every proposal that comes to them and to make recommendations to their boards about which proposals are creative and which fully represent the agencies' mission. You need to believe that your proposal will jump out of the reader's hands and take on a life of its own, that it will be so much more innovative than all the other proposals. Just nail down that idea first!

The SIGNALS Project

Keeping in mind adherence to your school's funding priorities, many schools have had considerable success with a grant project, then used that success to expand and enhance their original idea. One example of this is The SIGNALS Project. A group of middle school teachers met with me to discuss how they could obtain laptop computers for their science classrooms. Again, I was approached with a *need* for something, so I engaged them in thinking more about *ideas* that would serve to fulfill their need. I also asked them to investigate an educational problem they would solve with their idea.

Overview of Project

The project began by addressing two educational problems: the first dealt with the fact that females are underrepresented in the science-related fields; and the second dealt with the fact that schools located in isolated areas often do not have access to the same resources as those located in more urban settings. The teachers wanted laptops, complete with modems and telecommunications ability, so that they could break out of their rural setting and see what else was out there in the great big world. They talked about the most remote place they could go with the help of the Internet; a place so far removed from the Cornbelt that most students would never go there in their lifetimes. The result, after an entire year of planning and collaboration, was a direct telecommunicative relationship with the United States Coast Guard Ice Breaker *Polar Star*. The *Polar Star* ventures into the shipping lanes of the north and south poles, breaking ice so that safe passage is maintained for other vessels. The ship and her crew were more than willing to begin a relationship with this rather isolated middle school.

The school's staff also discovered that when the Coast Guard sails to these remote areas, their ships are laden with corps of scientists from various international laboratories and institutions. In fact, many of the Coast Guardsmen themselves are scientists and, to make things even better, a good majority of them are female! We had the makings of a great project here, since we had identified educational problems and were given the ideal setting in which to meet both.

The SIGNALS Projects (Supplemental Instruction for Girls in the Nautical Applications for Learning Science) was born in this highly collaborative and organized manner. Each year middle school-aged girls are able to join the SIGNALS Officer Corps, where they advance through a rank structure by managing the project, preparing presentations, partaking in science-related activities and bringing in female scientists to the school as guest speakers. The Officer Corps runs the show, and they are a highly efficient, quasi-military, all-female group that holds weekly uniformed inspections and expects the maintenance of a certain grade point average for each participant.

I've included The SIGNALS Project here, along with Project CROAK! in the Appendix, as excellent examples of how a needs-based approach to a grant can be turned around into an idea-based approach quite successfully. Both projects won the prestigious Pioneering Partners Award after their first year of implementation. The award is given throughout the eight Great Lakes States by The Council of Great Lakes Governors for innovative technology awards. From this base both projects have gone on to bring in considerable interest and funding from a variety of sources. Success attracts more success in the field of grants, and you must be ready for this when your creative idea is brought to life.

The SIGNALS Project went for years without any type of funding. The Officer Corps met several times after school and we conducted our activities throughout the school day. When we started getting small grants here and there, it made our activities that much easier to carry out, and we were able to attract more and more girls to the program. Now, after several grants and awards, the project is beginning to expand its relationships with female scientists in both the U.S. Coast Guard and U.S. Navy. Furthermore, having The SIGNALS Project in place in the middle school made our school district's acquisition of The JASON Project at the high school much easier. The JASON Project, led by noted oceanographer and scientist Dr. Robert Ballard, is an annual interactive exercise for students in undersea exploration and marine science. The grant cycle has proven very effective with this project. The original idea has been expanded upon each year, bringing more interest and resources.

Maureen McCune, Teacher/Director, The SIGNALS Project, Southport Middle School, Indianapolis, Indiana

Tips on Building Creativity

* **Read!** Periodicals that highlight creative approaches to existing educational problems include: *Instructor, T.H.E. Journal, Education Week,* and *The Chronicle of Philanthropy.* Skim these publications regularly to help spark creativity.

* **Collaborate with students, colleagues, parents, business leaders, and politicians.** Get their views on what they feel the important educational issues are. By soliciting advice from people outside the education field, you are demonstrating your professionalism.

* **Surf the Web.** Go beyond education-based Web sites—look at any kind of site that you think is fun and interesting. I often come across something on the Web that sparks an idea that becomes a classroom project. I'll give you

my favorite sites, but only if you'll promise to keep an open mind while visiting them:

http://www.killersites.com (Killer Web sites)
http://www.discovery.com (The Discovery Channel)
http://www.scholastic.com (Scholastic)
http://www.disney.com (Disney)
http://www.jasonproject.org (The Jason Project)
http://www.nasa.gov/ (NASA)
http://www.nsf.gov/ (National Science Foundation)

* **Use your pen!** The minute you see, hear, or read about great ideas, write them down. You may not need the ideas right away, but skimming through them once in a while may spark your own creativity. I do most of my thinking in my car, so I bring suction cup notepads to scribble in.

Chapter 2

Collaborating Counts

Collaboration is an essential ingredient of every grant proposal. Working with partners shows that you have confidence in your ideas and that you are willing to share them with others. Collaboration has many forms, but it mainly involves including qualified resources so that your project becomes the best it can be. Collaboration is sharing; it shows the funder that you are making a real effort to address an educational problem with an effective, creative solution that involves many different viewpoints.

Grant-based partnerships can become very productive over time, as long as each partner respects the others' talents, needs, interests and goals. It is quite refreshing to have capable individuals consulting grant recipients on items such as accounting methods, project design, client training, and program evaluation. Not only does the grant recipient benefit from collaboration, but the funder feels reassured that his grant is helping a school community work together to solve an educational problem.

Working Together on Small Grants

You can collaborate in many ways, depending upon the size and type of grant proposal you are writing. Let's say that the local United Way chapter is offering twenty-five grants of up to $2,500 for local school districts to address the problem of lack of interaction and sharing between schools and businesses. The United Way asks that submitting schools devise a creative approach to this problem, collaborating with as many resources as possible.

I would consider this a small grant opportunity, yet small grants are often the most important. Not only do they allow you to hone your proposal writing skills, but they also give you a reason to form relationships with individuals outside your school.

Here's how I would approach the United Way grant. To open up lines of communication between the community and school so that resources could be used to their fullest extent, I would establish an Internet directory, complete with e-mail addresses of all the parties involved in my project.

Most businesses have access to telecommunications. Most schools, unfortunately, don't. However, if we were to ask ten major businesses to establish

> You will be amazed at how much local and regional people can help you. Get them to talk with you about your project or write letters of support. They don't have to give you money, but they do have to buy into your idea. They can help set up training and facilities, loan or donate equipment, and offer their services at no cost. In the eyes of the funders, all of this adds up.
>
> *Becky Rennicke, Teacher,*
> *Perham Schools,*
> *Perham, Minnesota*

Who to Call

Consider contacting a variety of people for your grant.

- **Local certified public accountants** can help you set up your budget and manage your grant funds using sound accounting procedure.
- **Public relations and advertising professionals** can help with the writing of project abstracts, press releases, brochures, and reports.
- **The business community in general** can provide conference call arrangements, large meeting facilities and equipment, telephone lines, training and development, and mentoring and/or tutoring.
- **Retired teachers** can help with evaluation and training plans, as well as overall project management.
- **Library personnel (both school and local)** know where to look when you're writing the needs assessment part of the proposal.
- **Parents** can help achieve project objectives by assisting participants, making phone calls during the day, and promoting the project at various venues.

e-mail relationships with our classrooms, we could draw upon their employees' expertise as we study mathematics (business or accounting departments), science (technical support or engineering departments), English (marketing or public relations), or technology (data processing). Each of the ten businesses could give us a "Question of the Week." Students would then use the Internet to research the answers. Finally, we would have a day when the e-mail resources visit the classroom as guests, so kids get to the see the real people.

We would take about $1,500 of the grant monies and share the cost of a laptop computer with our school district. The computer would be shared by classes so that everyone has a chance to collaborate with business people. The rest of the grant money may go for materials and supplies, software, postage, copying, or any number of smaller expenses.

You can see how a little brainstorming could lead to better ideas. As for collaboration, we've established relationships with at least ten businesses outside the school—not only the supervisors of these organizations, but also employees in different departments. I can assure you that these employees will talk about the project with friends and neighbors.

We've also collaborated with a computer vendor in purchasing a laptop; such people usually know about the different computer-based projects going on in your area. If there is a natural link between your project and that of another school, vendors will be the first to let you know.

Don't forget about collaborating with the funder. By giving you a grant, the United Way has agreed that your creative solution is worth a try and within its means to fund. If you understand this relationship, and if you provide the necessary reports on time, the United Way could prove to be a very valuable resource for you in the long run.

Working Together on Larger Grants

If you are seeking a larger grant for which extensive program design and evaluation is necessary, collaboration will be essential and widespread. For instance, you may want to seek out assistance from local colleges or universities in devising curriculum or evaluation plans. You could call on local businesses or accountants to help with your budget and accounting plans. Retired teachers or other professionals could play vital roles during the grant with help in training, consulting, designing, or evaluating. Parents, with their many talents and interests, are a wonderful resource. It is perfectly acceptable (unless stated otherwise in the grant's guidelines) to pay these individuals as part of the grant's budget. Many times, though, help is offered free—a way in which interested individuals and companies show support for their schools.

It is wonderful to have unlimited resources available to you for grant projects, but it is also possible to have too many. It would be unwise, for instance, to have individuals from five universities working out an evaluation plan for your grant. Professionals often have different and competing views, and you will be placed into a position of deciding which view has the most relevance. Choose someone with talents you need, ask her to be a collaborator on your project, then give her the leverage she needs to accomplish her task. Remember: *You* have provided the vision, so *you* provide the leadership.

Enlisting Help

When you approach a potential collaborator for assistance, it is wise to be prepared and well informed.

- Sound excited about your creativity and your excitement will rub off.
- Explain the grant opportunity and the amount you will request.
- Outline the problem that the grant addresses and describe your creative solution.
- Ask the resource to join your team. Be specific about what you want her to do. If she accepts, make sure you commit her on the spot by giving her a meeting schedule, list of duties, and plan of action. If she wants to think about her commitment, thank her for considering your request, and set a time that you will get back to her. If she refuses, be gracious and ask if she would recommend someone else in her place. I make it a point to ask those who refuse if I may call on them for future projects to gauge their level of interest.

Chapter 3

The Importance of Starting Small

The most successful grant projects start with little or no funding. A group of teachers may come up with a creative project to do in the classroom, then realize their idea uniquely addresses an educational problem. They further develop their idea and decide to apply to their local education or community foundation for a small grant. They receive $250 toward supplies that will make their project easier to implement. They write a press release. They invite the funder to visit their school. Word gets around and before the teachers know it, the local manufacturer's CEO is offering a $1,000 grant to expand the project if the school's PTA kicks in $500. The teachers decide to develop the project district-wide, and receive large-scale funding for their efforts.

Here's how one teacher recognized the importance of starting from a single small idea:

> I applied for a grant from our local education foundation to purchase a computerized infant doll that would help middle-school students understand the vast responsibilities of teenage parenthood. My application was for $500. One of the foundation board members was the program officer for a local health foundation. She liked the project so much that her foundation purchased six dolls for my classroom, rather than one. The next year my project led to a grant from the state's Department of Health to purchase even more dolls. My local molehill turned into a statewide mountain very quickly. But I had prepared by enlisting as many parents and volunteers as I could. Today my school has an entire program set up for students to take the dolls home for long periods of time. This way, they really get an idea of what it's like to care for an infant and do well in school.
>
> *Denise Musick, Teacher*
> *Southport Middle School, Indianapolis, Indiana*

Your small grant can also turn into a large grant, if you want it to. Spread the word by bringing in the media and telling your story at school board and PTA meetings. In time, someone will take a keen interest in your efforts and offer services, money, or time. These elements help a project and are important to a funder who wonders whether or not your school and its community support what you're doing. Never underestimate the power of networking and marketing your work. The benefits of these activities may not be immediate or tangible, but they are more valuable than any grant you will ever receive.

You may decide not to pursue larger grants. You may not want to develop your projects into expansive undertakings. That $100 to purchase a set of books or that $1,000 to buy a drum set for the jazz band will suit you just fine. This type of funding is sometimes considered a grant, but it is really a gift, a wonderful thing. I urge you to apply for gifts. You receive them not necessarily because you have developed a creative approach to a problem or issue, but because you have convinced the funder you have a need. The momentum of a gift stops upon its receipt, while the momentum of a creative grant project never stops. It grows and grows as more people become aware of its impact, and the money continues to flow as funders scramble to be a part of your success.

Those who are not prepared for this momentum may want to reconsider starting their projects at all. It never looks good for a teacher or a school to have a grant project die, simply because no one has the time or inclination to carry on with the management, promotion, and collaboration required as a result of its expansion. If you receive a small grant that is truly a grant, and not a gift, then you must prepare for the growth of your project because it will surely come.

Many times teachers ask me, "What if I just want to go it alone and get small grants for my own classroom projects?" This is what many teachers choose to do. Small grants can help you obtain special equipment and supplies for your classroom; they can help launch that project you've always wanted to do; or they can help offset the cost of attending professional development conferences. If someone wants to give away computers, or underwrite attendance to a conference on a warm tropical island, or supply the school with a lifetime supply of CD-ROMs. . . that's OK! If *you* don't apply for these grants, I certainly will.

A Sample of Small Grants

Even small amounts of money require large amounts of creativity. Always aim for innovation in your approach. You *will* receive funding.

Success City

Amount of Grant: $500

The *Success City* project turns an empty classroom into a real-world setting that helps special education children gain knowledge of the proper behaviors within different types of environments. Third-, fourth- and fifth-grade students experience working in a bank, grocery store, hospital, and post office; live in each section of the city to prepare themselves for using these establishments in the future; and earn a salary, which teaches them about money management, paying bills, and being consumers.

Mother Goose on the Loose

Amount of Grant: $200

Mother Goose on the Loose helps students become better readers by teaching them about newspapers. The project shows students the difference between fact and opinion, examines research topics, investigates decision-making techniques, and closely scrutinizes newspaper art and graphic design. As the project ends, students write new versions of the Mother Goose nursery rhymes in a newspaper format.

Backpack Science

Amount of Grant: $500

The *Backpack Science* project enhances and supplements the science curriculum for grades one through five. It encourages children and their parents to collaborate on a prescribed activity at home. Students take prepared science experiments home in a backpack and, with the help of their parents, complete the experiments and record the data. At school, the children chart, graph, and summarize results of their experiments.

Wisconsin Fast Plants

Amount of Grant: $500

Fourth-grade students investigate plant growth and development, life spirals, and ecology using *Wisconsin Fast Plants* as living models. These rapid-cycling plants have unique properties that make them ideally suited for a six-week unit that emphasizes plants. Students use scientific method and reasoning, and discover the importance of pollination in the plant reproductive cycle. They are also able to identify plant and flower parts.

Basic Skills III

Amount of Grant: $500

The *Basic Skills III* project is a grant-supported course offered to all high school students for credit. The course covers the conflicts and dilemmas that African-American males face. It also introduces students to African-American writers. Community leaders and mentors come into the classroom as discussion leaders and role models.

Parents as Partners

Amount of Grant: $500

Parents as Partners provides opportunities for parents of elementary school students to interact with other parents and teachers as they study and discuss learning and guidance. Workshops are provided for the introduction and discussion of ideas and school-related problems. Also, a library has been established from which parents may check out books and videos on topics such as discipline, self- and home-esteem, parenting, and how to handle attention deficit children.

Chapter 4

Grant Writing as a Team

Just as collaboration is essential to grants, so is teamwork. You may become interested in a grant opportunity and gather other interested teachers and administrators. You may involve parents and actively seek outside collaborators. Or you may devise a creative solution to an educational problem. In all these cases, you are building a grant writing team based on organization, inspiration, leadership, creativity, and a variety of professional skills.

With most grant projects someone takes the helm and represents the group. But when all of the duties of a project end up in the lap of one person, then you are heading for problems. As you write grant proposals and receive funding, make a plan for sharing the tasks. Make one person responsible for sending reports and updates to the funder. Another person might answer all inquiries regarding your project and its success. Have at least one troubleshooter around to keep the project's objectives and activities on track. Also, have a core of people who specialize in maintaining smooth implementation of the project and don't have to worry about all the peripheral distractions. In some cases there won't be this many people to share the duties. Delegate tasks as best you can, and be firm to your supervisors about your needs for assistance.

Form a Grant Team

The best way to obtain grants is to establish a school-based Grant Team. Before the team takes the field, however, your school must decide what types of grants it will pursue. For instance, a school may decide that technology, geography, and international studies are topics of interest. The team will target grant opportunities that support these areas.

As the team works to put the grant proposal together, and when (not *if*) the project is actually funded, you will notice that each team member has become an arc in the grant circle. Within the circle, team member duties meld into one another so that the team, like the process itself, become an interdependent set of gears that produce ideas, seek collaborative relationships, search for funding, organize implementation, then refocus again on the manufacture of ideas.

The Grant Researcher

- **Begins the search**
- **Compiles the data**

As the lead person of the grant team, the grant researcher must know about written and online resources for grants. Her name must be on the mail-

ing list of several funding agencies, and she must possess an extensive list of Web sites that focus on grant opportunities. The grant researcher must learn to be very picky and has to be willing to let certain grant opportunities go even if they seem too good to be true. Her objective is to find grants for projects that the school has targeted. For instance, she may be directed to find grants that address female underrepresentation in science, failing test scores in social studies, and the lack of higher-education resources for elementary and secondary students. She must focus on those subjects. The school can always change its mind about priorities.

Someone with Access

Often, the media specialist or someone with access to research materials becomes the grant researcher. Several publications list education grants, but many are too expensive for school budgets and may list grants with imminent deadlines. Other resources list federal, foundation, and corporation programs, but these publications are usually located in city or county libraries rather than in schools. Finally, as access to technology becomes more common, many funders turn to this paperless way of announcing grants.

All information comes in handy sometime. The grant researcher should keep records of all grant opportunities that may be of interest to her school, now or in the future. Many grant programs are annual, so even though there may not be enough time to apply for one this year, the researcher can devise an early-warning system for next year. Administrators must understand that researching grants is like researching anything else—it takes time. The benefits of allowing the grant researcher to spend a day at the public library every month will far outweigh the costs of providing her substitute. Because many funders announce their grants on Web sites, having access to the Internet is relatively low cost and essential.

The Grant Analyst

- **Refines the search**
- **Follows up leads**
- **Makes good matches**
- **Channels information**

The grant analyst takes the grant researcher's information and seeks additional, more detailed information from the funder. Many grant opportunities are announced with little information. Complete applications and guidelines usually have to be requested in a more detailed manner. The grant researcher may be able to ascertain if a particular opportunity falls within the school's funding priorities. But the grant analyst must take that determination one step further with a full-blown investigation.

The analyst contacts the potential funder by telephone, FAX, e-mail, or pre-proposal letter (whichever the funder prefers). He must follow instructions exactly. If the funder says "no telephone calls," then don't call.

By asking for a pre-proposal or pre-proposal letter, the funder provides a chance to summarize the project before the full proposal is sent out, which can save valuable time. Pre-proposal letters are a wonderful trend in the grant writing industry and are quickly replacing other forms of first communication with funders. The letters are usually two pages long and include an abstract of the project, a timeline, and the total amount requested. Pre-proposal letters must also briefly mention your project goal, objectives, and activities. Funders will review your pre-proposal information and quickly (usually within a few weeks) let you know if the relationship should continue.

Saying What They Mean

Analyzing grant information can be tricky. Funders don't often mince words in their guidelines and applications. What they say or write is what they mean. Most grants accurately reflect the information provided. But sometimes the full information packet contains surprises. The analyst will be sure to check for matching fund requirements, local resource commitments, eligibility, reporting procedures, and methods for actually obtaining the grant funds. Before going any further the grant analyst will be certain that the grant opportunity and the funder are the right match for his school community. If for some reason they are not, he should immediately look for other sources of funding. By being selective, the grant analyst will be doing himself and the funder a big favor in the long run.

The grant analyst is the funnel for information to the rest of the grant team. He sorts through complete information about grant opportunities before submitting his findings to the rest of the group. The grant team trusts him to root out any loopholes in grant opportunities before a commitment is made. Most importantly, the grant team realizes that not all grant opportunities will yield funding, regardless of the amount of research that has gone into choosing the right funder. The team knows, from the very beginning, that it is more productive to pursue grants for projects in which the school has an interest and which have the best chance for success. An organized approach to finding grants proves your team's competency. It can result in endless resources for your school.

The Profiler

✻ Maintains files of basic information

✻ Updates important school information every year

✻ Always has information available

The profiler knows more about the school and community than anyone else on the grant team. She is responsible for collecting and constantly updating boilerplate information for grant proposals. Boilerplate files include

- school demographics
- student racial make-up
- staff characteristics
- building assets
- active organizations
- enrollment figures
- socio-economic status
- financial data
- prior grants and awards
- special school designations

Any information that rarely changes during the school year is fodder for the profiler. Not all of this information may be used in a grant proposal, but it's good to have it available.

The Assessor

- ❊ **Targets one area of a grant**
- ❊ **Focuses on research**
- ❊ **Saves information**

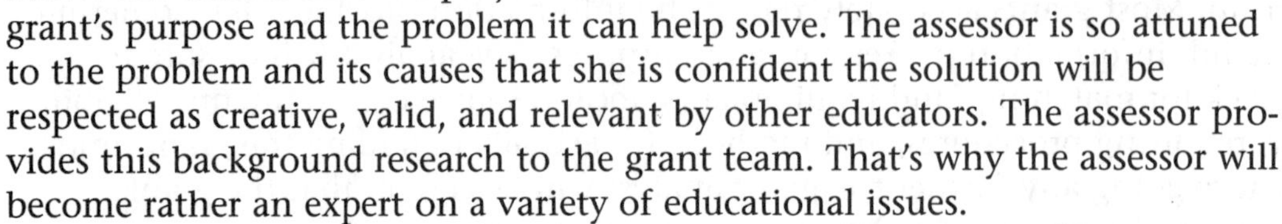

The assessor refers to the Needs Assessment or Problem Statement portion of a grant proposal. The assessor knows that this information is of vital importance. It shows the funder that the project staff understands the grant's purpose and the problem it can help solve. The assessor is so attuned to the problem and its causes that she is confident the solution will be respected as creative, valid, and relevant by other educators. The assessor provides this background research to the grant team. That's why the assessor will become rather an expert on a variety of educational issues.

The assessor spends a good deal of time in the library and online. She must scan a lot of information, choosing what is relevant and applicable to the grant project. The assessor is always on the lookout for interesting and usable quotations, theories, previous studies and their results, and statistics. By doing this, she:

- shows the team and the funder why, how, and what the grant will help.
- demonstrates to the funder what attempts were made in the past to solve the problem the grant is meant to address.
- creates a list of sources relevant to the problem for other educators to use now or in the future.

A wise assessor keeps all research information, regardless of how useful it may be to the grant proposal. She never knows when the need for data or information may arise. One day, the focus of this research may become a "hot" grant topic and the research will become a wonderful source for background review.

The Collaboration Manager

- ❊ **Communicates with outside support**
- ❊ **Conveys positive spirit**

Because working as a team to create and develop grant projects is essential, the collaboration manager is the person who leads that effort. She starts relationships with parents, business leaders, politicians, and other community members. Then she nurtures and maintains them. She is the point person between the school and the outside world. She must know who supports the schools and who would be willing to help with a grant project. And since every resource cannot be used on every project, she must keep up relationships with her contacts even if she's not working with them at the moment.

The collaboration manager must work closely with the entire team so that she can keep partners up to date. Many of these partners won't be able to meet during normal business or school hours, so the school must be flexible.

In most cases, partners will provide their services free of charge as a way of showing support for education. Sometimes, though, paying a partner with grant funds is necessary and proper. The collaboration manager is responsible for researching current rates for services and then negotiating the partner's payment.

A collaboration manager should not be discouraged if, after going to great lengths to establish a partnership, the grant proposal is denied. She must make it clear that grants are competitive, but she must display confidence that her team's proposal will be funded. If it is not, she must explain to partners that the team believes in the project enough to resubmit the proposal to another funder. The collaboration manager should keep partners in the loop on her progress. She must welcome all partners into the school's family and infect them with the contagious enthusiasm that keeps the creative project moving forward for the entire team.

My Favorite Research

I enjoy the needs assessment research of any grant proposal because I love to learn. The most extensive needs assessment research I ever did was in response to a National Science Foundation program addressing the problem of female underrepresentation in the fields of science, mathematics, and engineering. I spent a considerable amount of time skimming over the early, basic texts and research to get a grasp of the problem. I then focused on more recent articles in educational periodicals and journals. Finally, I did concentrated searches over the Internet and found the e-mail addresses of experts in the field.

I used about one quarter of my research in the actual grant proposal, but felt I had learned a lot about the subject, knowledge I shared with the rest of the group.

While I researched the issue of female underrepresentation in science, I found myself reading opinions not only from experts in the science fields, but also from those in the fields of psychology, social science, anthropology, and history. Our grant project dealt with changing the attitudes and perceptions of the science field to young women, rather than with a more tangible issue such as test scores. My research found that, in fact, there is little difference between the science test scores of males and females (at least in middle school), but there are substantial differences in attitudes and perceptions toward science. These conclusions helped shape our project and make our objectives more relevant.

The assessor's job is my favorite. Faced with the task of proving to a funder that I understand the educational problem, and then providing a creative approach to the problem's solution is an exhilarating and inspirational process. The assessor is exposed to interesting issues; I opted to further investigate them on my own for my own growth.

—Dennis M. Norris

The Editor

- **Writes clearly and concisely**
- **Keyboards**
- **Maintains schedule**

Many pieces of writing go into a grant proposal. The person who does that writing, the editor, needs a sharp grasp of grammar, punctuation, and syntax and the ability to describe your program clearly and concisely. The editor must also be a diplomat, skilled at editing while being sensitive to the feelings of other team members.

Editing and writing and keyboarding is a lot of time-consuming work. The collaboration manager might suggest someone outside the school who can help out—a parent or retired teacher, for example. Whoever does this vital job must know desktop publishing. That's essential.

The editor is also the keeper of schedules. Too many grant proposals are finished the night before the deadline. A good editor keeps the team appraised of deadlines and requests progress reports.

The Business Manager

- **Oversees money matters**
- **Advises on costs**

The business manager is another important team member. His support is needed from the very beginning to advise the team on strategies for accepting, spending, and reporting on grant funds. He may also help with the proposal budget and, as is often required by funders, prepare audit materials to send along with the proposal.

The business manager is usually the actual business manager for the school district; he knows about your state's public-school finance regulations. Most of these regulations apply to grant funds, and the grant team must be aware of the level of accountability expected of them by the funder *and* by the state government.

The business manager can also help with the grant process by advising the team on "hidden" costs. For instance, if your grant budget contains salaries for individuals, the business manager can tell you how much to figure in for retirement, taxes, or other monies that must be withheld. He may also know of vendors that will offer the school special discounted rates for equipment or services. If any type of insurance is required, the business manager can speak with the school district's insurance company to determine whether considerable savings can be had by attaching riders to existing policies. Finally, the business manager can often field those hard-to-answer financial questions about shared expense, matching funds, budget transfers, and reporting procedures for which funders ask.

The Superintendent

- **Provides moral and material support**
- **Networks**

The top administrator of your school district should know about your grant writing efforts and should provide support for your project in the form of teacher release time, substitutes, stipends, equipment, or professional development costs.

Administrative support in any form is necessary for a successful proposal. Most funders prefer financial support, they see it as an in-kind contribution on the proposal budget.

Attaching a letter of support from the superintendent to a grant proposal is a good idea. This tells the funder that the grant writing effort is not a localized effort, that it is the work of many individuals taking place over several weeks or months. A letter of support shows the school's administration is aware of these efforts. The superintendent is stating his or her belief in the power of creativity in solving educational problems. Coming from a school administrator, this is very powerful stuff.

When the superintendent buys into your project, the grant team knows it is undertaking an important task. The superintendent can get things done and has many community connections. The power of networking can never be underestimated, especially in creating and developing grants. Administrative support helps bring in outside resources and professionals.

The Parents

- **Share team tasks**
- **Network**

Parents know everybody! Here again, networking in the school community is a valuable activity. Another strength of parent involvement has to do with the nature of grants themselves. Once funded, teachers can count on spending a little more time before or after school for planning, training, implementing, or generally managing the grant. This can become rather tiring, so it is wise to include parents in the grant cycle from the very beginning. A teacher will have more confidence in a parent sharing tasks if the parent has been around and knows the grant's objectives.

The Developers

- **Pull process together**
- **Solicit support**
- **Produce proposal**

Though I have saved the developers of a grant team for last, they are its core. After all, someone has to pull together the project; someone has to write it. The developers include those with the original proposal idea, those who want to brainstorm and document the evolution of the idea into a grant proposal. Working with all other members of the team, the developers put into tangible form everything from plans of action to the writing of the proposal.

Developers must occasionally meet apart from other members of the team. After all, they take its work and put it to practical use. Developers take information from the assessor and the profiler, then incorporate it into the proposal. Developers also determine the objectives and activities of the proposal, keeping in mind the placement and duties of any collaborators. If outside partners are working on the proposal (such as trainers or evaluators), the developers must clearly outline the duties expected of each. When working with the business manger, superintendent, and parents, the developers must articulate the project and solicit support. Finally, the developers must work closely with the editor to meet all deadlines and produce quality prose.

When the project is funded, the developers become the implementors. They must switch roles from designing the

Work Flow

Grant Researcher
- Identifies basic information
- Turns information over to **Grant Analyst**

↓

Grant Analyst
- Prepares two-page pre-proposal letter to the **Funder**

↓

Funder
- Asks **Grant Team** for a full proposal

↓

Grant Team
- Asks **Profiler** to prepare boilerplate
- Gives **Assessor** one month to research educational problem

project and building interest to managing the project and maintaining interest. From implementors the group evolves further into disseminators. If your creative approach to an educational problem is an effective one, then it is your duty as an educator to disseminate it. Writing articles, attending conferences, or just spreading the word about your efforts is a part of your grant's success. Your story is best told by you, the persons responsible for the project from idea to implementation. Funders will appreciate your success because it is their success, too. In your dissemination efforts, never fail to mention where the support came from. A grant is a partnership between you and a funder, and it will increase your chances for even more funding if you give credit where credit's due.

Useful Resources

Throughout the United States there are Foundation Centers in libraries. They have the references, guidebooks, periodicals, and texts that I've been mentioning. Below I've listed The Foundation Center's four main offices. Call or write to them to find out where your nearest Foundation Center is located. They are certainly worth a visit. I've also listed a few of the resources available at The Foundation Center. For a more complete listing please check the Appendix.

The Foundation Center
79 Fifth Avenue
New York, NY 10003
(212) 620-4230

The Foundation Center
Kent H. Smith Library
1442 Hanna Building
1422 Euclid Avenue
Cleveland, OH 44115
(216) 861-1933

The Foundation Center
1001 Connecticut Ave. NW
Washington, DC 20036
(201) 331-1400

The Foundation Center
312 Sutter Street
San Francisco, CA 94108
(415) 397-0902

Some resources you will find at The Foundation Center:

- *Federal Grants and Contracts Weekly*—Weekly profiles of various federal grant opportunities.
- *Education Grants Alert*—Weekly profiles of education grants from federal, foundation and corporate funders.
- *Getting Grants* by Craig Smith and Eric Skjei. An overview of getting federal grants with some sample proposals.
- *Grants for Teachers* by Jacqueline Ferguson. Anything Ms. Ferguson writes, you should read. This book lists hundreds of grants, awards, and fellowships for teachers.
- *America's Newest Foundations*, a resource manual that profiles foundations formed during the last five years and what types of grants they give.
- *The Foundation Directory*, a Foundation Center resource that lists more than 4,400 foundations and their giving histories.
- *Taft Foundation Reporter*, a profile of more than 500 private foundations and the types of grants they award.
- *Taft Corporate Giving Directory*, lists corporate giving programs and their grants.

Chapter 5

Grants, Grants, Everywhere!

You've got a great idea, you've gathered together a network of collaborators, and you've established a grant team within your school. All you need now are grant opportunities. Where will they come from? Will people come knocking at your door with their pockets filled with money? Must you commit every waking hour to soliciting funders? How will you find out about those big grant opportunities before it's too late?

Fear not. There are plenty of ways to find out about grants. But, because grants come in two varieties, reactive and proactive, you must understand the characteristics of both before you can proceed. Reactive and proactive grants have the same value. But, depending on the parameters of your project and how much money you're trying for, one type may have a slight advantage over the other. That is why you must know about each type. Neither is easier to write or manage than the other. The basic grant writing ideas in this book will help you pursue either one. This is yet another reason why I enjoy writing grant proposals so much. Not only can I be creative and work with others who also care about educating kids, but I can also shop around for the right funder or the right funding situation. It is truly a science of matching your goals with those of a funder. The variety of funders makes the search half the fun.

Reactive Grants

Those hundreds of grant opportunities you hear about in publications, magazines, bulletins and over the Internet are reactive grants. The federal or state government, private or public foundation, corporate giving organizations or private citizens have announced the availability of funds to solve certain educational problems. Cursory information is outlined in these announcements—usually enough for you to determine whether or not the grant is one your school wants to try for.

What Funders Tell You

1. Name of the program and name of the funding organization
2. Brief description of the grant and its aim
3. Eligibility requirements for applicants
4. Amount of grant or a range within which the grant budget must remain
5. Timeline for grant to be completed
6. Deadline for the proposal or pre-proposal or other information regarding how to proceed.
7. What is available with the grant: equipment, supplies, training, online services

8. Contact name, address, telephone number, FAX number, and e-mail address.

A typical reactive grant announcement may look like this:

> The XYZ Foundation announces the Students Against Violence Program to address the problem of violence in schools. Projects should concentrate on promoting self-esteem and peer counseling to students, rather than purchasing metal detectors or security services. This is a one-year grant program available to public school districts or nonprofit educational organizations. Collaboration with outside organizations is highly preferred.
>
> Fifty grants are available of up $25,000 each. Grant recipients will also be given access to the XYZnet Internet server for one year so that dissemination and collaboration may take place among the awardees. Applicants must submit a two-page pre-proposal by September 15, 1998, briefly listing their project objectives, list of collaborators and budget. The foundation will notify those applicants they wish to continue with the application process by October 15, 1998. The finalists will be asked to complete a full proposal by December 15, 1998.
>
> To obtain an application or for further information contact Phil Anthropy, Program Officer, XYZ Foundation, 1111 Main Street, Grant, USA 12345, (123)456-7890, FAX (123)456-7891, e-mail: panthropy@xyznet.com.

If one of your school's funding priorities is violence in schools, then you probably have a bank of creative ideas that could be used to address the problem. In fact, these creative ideas should already have been developed, along with support from the school and community. They are ideas waiting for a funding opportunity to which you would "react."

If your creative ideas to the problem fits within the funder's framework, then you should apply for the grant. You may have to tweak your project a bit to make it fit someone else's guidelines. It will be your decision on how much you do or do not want to change the original idea. Sometimes it is worth it, other times it is not. Your own experience will help you decide.

My personal rule is to go for a reactive grant opportunity as long as it doesn't take away from the original creativity or original objectives of the project. I probably miss out on a lot of grants by being this stubborn, but there are thousands of reactive and proactive grant opportunities out there. My preference would be to find a funder whose guidelines match my project rather than to change my project to fit a funder's guidelines.

Where to Find Reactive Grants

- *Education Grants Alert* (Capitol Publications, [800] 655-5597), is a weekly publication that provides details on new and recent grants.
- *Catalog of Federal Domestic Assistance*, published by the U.S. government, is a guide to all federal reactive grants. It can be found in most large public libraries or online at http://www.gsa.gov/fdac/
- Periodicals such as *The Chronicle of Philanthropy, Education Week,* or *T.H.E. Journal* frequently list reactive grants.

* Here are some of the better reactive grant Web sites:

http://www.adobe.com/aboutadobe/philanthropy/main.html/ (Adobe)
http://www.americanexpress.com/corp/philanthropy/ (American Express)
http://www.ameritech/com/news/contributions/index.html/ (Ameritech)
http://www.att.com/foundation/ (AT&T)
http://www.benjerry.com/foundation.html/ (Ben & Jerry's)
http://cio.cisco.com/jobs/community.html/ (Cisco)
http://www.digital.com:80/info/community/contribu.html (Digital)
http://www.gte.com/Glance/Business/Service/Docs/found.html/ (GTE)
http://www.corp.hp.com/Publish/UG/ (Hewlett-Packard)
http://www.ibm.com/IBM/IBMGives/ (IBM)
http://www.intel.com/intel/smithso/community.htm/ (Intel)
http://www.kodak.com:80/aboutKodak/corpinto/community.html (Kodak)
http://www.mitsubishi.com/groups/meaf.htm/ (Mitsubishi)
http://www.sega.com/world/foundation/ (Sega)
http://www.wal-mart.com/ (Wal Mart)
http://www.ed.gov/ (Education Department)
http://www.os.dhhs.gov/ (Health & Human Services)
http://www.epa.gov/ (Environmental Protection Agency)
http:/www.ims.fed.us/ (Institute of Museum Services)
http://www.nasa.gov/ (NASA)
http://www.arts.endow.gov/ (NEA)
http://www.neh.fed.us/ (NEH)
http://www.nsf.gov/ (NSF)
http://infoserv.rttonet.psu.edu/ (GrantsWeb)
http://www.access.gpo.gov/su_docs/ (Federal Register)

Proactive Grants

There are times when you have such a terrific creative idea that you just can't sit around and wait for a reactive grant opportunity. That's fine. You don't have to. Thousands of organizations in the United States that have educational grants available announce their funding in appropriate publications, then wait for *you* to contact *them*. This is the proactive way to get grants.

Many libraries across the nation have listings of foundations and corporations. These are the best resources for proactive grant information. The entries not only list current grant information, but also information on funded projects from previous years. Each organization will state its own funding priorities, which are often general and broad in scope. Your creative project can usually fit under any number of these guidelines, which you can find under "education."

Proactive funding organizations have the right to be picky about what they fund, since they have not tied themselves down to more specific reactive grant guidelines. You must take the responsibility for determining whether or not your project interests the funder. This can often be accomplished by a telephone call or pre-proposal. If the interest is there, you will be recontacted by the organization and asked to submit either a full proposal or further, more detailed information. Communication with proactive grant funders is generally quick, allowing you the opportunity to move ahead with the relationship or to seek another funder.

A typical proactive funder announcement may look like this:

The XYZ Foundation is a family-owned philanthropic institution that has been supporting creative approaches to problems in education, religion and the social sciences for the past one hundred years. Funding priority is given first to educational projects supporting K–8 education, secondly to projects promoting religious diversity, and lastly to projects supporting research in the social sciences. The board of directors consists of the XYZ family members, and meets quarterly to make funding decisions.

For an annual report and a listing of funded projects over the last five years, please leave a voicemail message at (123) 555-7890. Parties interested in funding should first contact John Doe, Program Officer, at the above number to discuss your project.

Where to Find Proactive Grant Resources

- *Foundation and Corporate Grants Alert* (Capitol Publications, [800] 655-5597), a monthly publication, describes the philanthropic interests of foundations and corporations.
- Catalogs such as *The Directory of Corporate and Foundation Givers, The Foundation Reporter,* and *The Foundation Directory* allow you to look up funders by name, subject matter, or geographical location. The Foundation Directory (The Foundation Center, [800] 424-9836); The Directory of Corporate and Foundation Givers and The Foundation Reporter (Taft Corporation, [800] 877-8238), are available at larger public libraries and libraries that house Foundation Centers. Call (800) 424-9836 to find out the Foundation Center nearest you.
- The best proactive Web sites are:
  - http://www.ingress.com/amc/grants.html/ (American Music Center)
  - http://www.carnegie.org/ (Andrew Carnegie Foundation)
  - http://www.dana.org/ (Charles A. Dana Foundation)
  - http://www.ef.org/ (Energy Foundation)
  - http://www.heinz.org/menu.html/ (Heinz Endowments)
  - http://www.rwjf.org/ (Robert Wood Johnson Foundation)
  - http://www.glef.org/ (George Lucas Educational Foundation)
  - http://www.macfdn.org/ (John D. & Catherine T. MacArthur Foundation)
  - http://www.nsta.org/programs/ (NSTA)
  - http://www.pewtrusts.com/ (Pew Charitable Trusts)
  - http://www.silcom.com/weboflight/ (Points of Light Foundation)
  - http://www.turnerfoundation.org/ (Turner Foundation)
  - http://www.cof.org/ (Council of Foundations)
  - http://www.fdncenter.org/ (Foundation Center)
  - http://www.technogrants.com/2.htm/ (Foundations)
  - http://www.indepsec.org/ (Independent Sector)

Once you decide where you will locate grant information, you must create a way to manage the information. Many grants come around the same time every year. It helps to keep grant information on file or in a database for five or six years. What you may pass on this year could be useful next year. If you already have the information and if you've checked to make sure the grant is still being offered, then you've got a jump on preparing your project.

Keeping Track over Time

Whenever I come across a reactive grant opportunity I look at its deadline month, then I subtract eight months, and place this date under a column called "Notify." Of course, I also enter other important information, such as the program name, funding agency, and the amount of the grant. I also have a coded system that tells me where I found the grant information in case I want to go back and look at it more closely.

The Notify column is important to me because at the first of each month I call up this information. For example, if a reactive grant opportunity has a deadline of January 15, then I enter May in the Notify column of my database. The month of May is eight months prior to January. When May 1 comes around, I sort my Notify column so that all of the January grant opportunities are presented to me eight months before their deadline. Sure, some grants don't come around every year, and some don't keep the same guidelines or exact deadline dates. But in May you can believe I'm calling the different January funders and asking them if they plan to do the same grant program with the same basic guidelines. If they are, then I have six or seven months to get my grant team going to produce a great proposal.

PROGRAM NAME	AMOUNT	AGENCY	CONTACT	DEADLINE	NOTIFY
Parents and Children for Terrific Science	$1,200	American Chemical Society 1155 16th Street NW Washington, DC 20036.	Ann Benhow (202) 452-2113	MAR 31	JUL
American Heroes in Education Award	$15,000	Reader's Digest Pleasantville, NY 10572	Mary Terry (914) 238-1000	NOV	MAR
Christa McAuliffe Awards	$1,000	National Council for Social Studies 3501 Newark Street NW Washington, DC 20016	Program Officer (202) 966-7840	APR 1 odd years	AUG even years
GIFT Program (Growth Initiatives for Teachers)	$12,000	GTE Foundation 1 Stamford Forum Stamford, CT 06904	Maureen Gorman, Vice President (203) 965-3620	JAN	MAY
Just Do It Teachers' Grants	$5,000– $25,000	Dropout Prevention Program 1201 16th Street NW Washington, DC 20036	Program Officer (202) 822-7840	FEB	JUN

Managing proactive grant information is slightly different, since proposal deadlines vary considerably based on the meeting schedule of the organization's board of directors. Because of this, I sort proactive funders under a column called Priority. I research proactive funders who have funding priorities under headings such as education, technology, literacy, violence in school, environmental education, vocational education, special education.

Periodically, or when I have a grant project that doesn't seem to fit a reactive opportunity because of its complexity or dollar range, I sort my Priority column by the topic I'm interested in. As you can imagine, I am constantly adding to this database as I learn about new funding agencies. On the other hand, I am constantly revising this database as well, since some corporate funders seem to change their funding priorities quite often. One reason for this is that many corporations set up funding groups that are run by a board of employees. The employees serve for one or two years. They vote on funding

priorities during their terms. When they leave and new employees take their place, the funding priorities may change.

Keeping up with these changes can be a chore, but it is worth it. The best way is to get on the organization's mailing list and to read its literature each year. Sooner or later a corporate giver will have the same priorities as your school.

Warning!

Sometimes grants come up that seem too good to pass by. It's fine to indulge yourself once in awhile, but too much of a good thing can be dangerous. Stick to your school's funding priorities or you will find yourself in a disjointed, unorganized feeding frenzy on all of those quick and easy grants. They may bring in money and equipment to your school for the short term, but in the long term they undermine the confidence you've built up in your collaborators, parents, and other supporters. It is much better to stick to your priorities, work over time on creative approaches, build a support network, and research a funding match that will have true longevity and mutual support.

Important: One at a Time

Submit your proposal to only one funder at a time. This is an unwritten rule in grant writing. Not following it can quickly earn your school a bad reputation. Funders assume that you have researched them as a good match for your ideas, and that you are sincerely interested in them as a partner in your efforts. The philanthropic community is very close. Don't put yourself in an awkward position by saturating the market with your proposal.

Suppose you are tying to obtain shared grant support from a number of agencies for the same project. By all means send your proposal to each of the sharing partners. However, make certain that you tell each organization that you have sent the same document to the others, and that your hope is to establish a comprehensive, shared relationship with them all.

Chapter 6

Writing the Proposal

Your proposal not only documents ideas, but is often the first impression that a funder receives. A growing number of funders simply ask for a ten-page proposal. They won't tell you what to write in those ten pages—they'll assume you already know. If you know the basic elements of a grant proposal and provide them as requested, you will show the funder that you are competent and ready to implement all aspects of your project.

When you write the proposal elements, keep these general rules in mind.

* **Stay away from educational jargon.** Not everyone knows about metacognitive learning and Bloom's Taxonomy. Be simple, be clear, and assume your reader has no prior knowledge of your project or field of expertise.
* **Just give the facts.** Stay away from value judgments, such as "Our school is just great," and "Our project director is one of the most inspirational and dedicated educators to ever grace the halls of this school." Just give the funder the facts without all the glitter.
* **Give the funders what they ask for.** If they want ten pages, give them ten pages. If five of those pages should be objectives, give them five pages of objectives. If guidelines for writing the proposal are not stated, prepare a proposal that is properly weighted and professionally written. Don't try to make a good impression with things that aren't asked for, such as fancy graphics or expensive paper. It will almost surely backfire.
* **Practice what you preach to your students.** Follow directions and do what you are told!

Parts of a Proposal

1. Summary

Also called *abstract*; one-page review of project that goes on top of the proposal, usually without a page number (see Appendix B for model).

A. Contents

a. project goal
b. objectives
c. activities
d. evaluation plan
e. timeline
f. dollar amount

B. Qualities

a. brevity
b. clarity
c. serves as an informational piece for funders
d. could be turned into public relations release when funding occurs

2. *Introduction*

The place to toot your school's horn

A. **Contents**

- **a.** school demographics and socio-economic figures
- **b.** staff accomplishments or awards
- **c.** school's previous grant projects (short list!)

B. **Qualities**

- **a.** content should be relevant to grant you are seeking
- **b.** accurate picture of school
- **c.** establishes credibility and illuminates school's accomplishments

EXAMPLE: A one-paragraph introduction

The Cool School District is located within the Golden Valley, in the northern part of the state. Students attending the district are generally from homes of middle- to high socioeconomic status. The demographic makeup of the district is 80 percent white and 20 percent African- American. PTA membership has set the state record for the past five years, and PTA funds have allowed the district to put advanced telecommunications cabling into each elementary school. In anticipation of receiving grant funding for telecommunications-based projects, the Cool School District staff has undergone extensive training on the use of telecommunications in the classroom and its integration into the curriculum. The students, parents, teachers and business community are trained and prepared to take the next steps in bringing technological innovation to the Golden Valley.

3. *Needs Assessment*

States the problem

A. **Contents**

- **a.** explains educational problem
- **b.** offers backup: current research, quotes, statistics, and studies, all valid and reliable

B. **Qualities**

- **a.** starts with general information, then becomes more specific
- **b.** provides background on the problem—what has or hasn't been done to solve it.

EXAMPLE: A needs assessment

With the American history problem, I would most likely look for research telling me that ignorance of basic historical facts hurts us as a nation. I would find some good quotes by prominent historians or politicians. Next I would contact my state's Department of Education to determine what the statewide test scores tell about knowledge of history hoping for a quote from the top social studies person or the superintendent of schools. Last, I would concentrate on my own region, school district and school in order to "localize" the problem. Examining test scores, surveys, attitudes of teachers and parents, I would attempt to show how this national problem finds its way to the classroom level.

4. *Objective*

Outcomes

A. Contents

a. lists learning games, attitude shifts, increased test scores, or an end product

b. presents data that project produced

B. Qualities

a. tells *who* is going to do *what, when* they are going to do it, and *how* it can be measured

b. has just the right amount of listed outcomes: three to five for medium-sized proposals and ten to fifteen for larger proposals. Too few indicate a lack of direction, too many will bog you down.

EXAMPLE: There are many different types of objectives, and it is a risky prospect to offer you examples. Objectives are what's left over after the project has been implemented and is long gone. Your objectives are the next set of data for future grant writers. I can assure you that years from now someone will look at your project and the data you produced, add their own special creative touch, and come up with an entirely different approach.

Yes!

At the conclusion of the five-day workshop [**when**], at least 75 percent of the project participants [**who**] will demonstrate a pre- and post-test [**how measured**] knowledge gain regarding the use of technology in education and its direct application in the classroom [**what**].

No!

At the end of the workshop, project participants will understand how technology is used in the classroom.

Let's restate the "good" objective example used above, then list some activities:

Objectives:

At the conclusion of the five-day workshop, at least 75 percent of the project participants will demonstrate a pre- and post-test knowledge gain regarding the use of technology in education and its direct application in the classroom.

Activities:

1. A five-day workshop will be held in the school's media center during the second week in July. Participants will demonstrate their proficiency in gaining access to the Internet with the assistance of student coaches. Students will be utilized for this project as an innovative way to foster creative learning in adults and explore the reliability of simple approaches to seemingly complex activities.
2. During the first two days of the workshop, participants will be directed to several different online databases and Web pages by the coaches, and they will have ample time to browse and explore. Coaches will introduce teachers to their favorite Internet sites, and teachers will be able to gain a sense of what excites children and stimulates their learning.

3. On the third day of the workshop the coaches will administer a proficiency quiz to each participant, then all parties will meet in the afternoon to discuss the creation of an online classroom project that incorporates database searching. Student coaches will gain a sense of accomplishment by turning the tables and testing the teachers, and teachers will be able to take advantage of the "child's view" as they work on their creative classroom projects.
4. The fourth day of the workshop will be a free day, enabling teacher-coach teams to explore online and/or develop their projects. By this time in the workshop the coaches and teachers will have developed a close working and learning relationship. Together they will assist with one another's learning so they can learn more about technology and its potential use in the classroom.
5. As a culminating event to the workshop, each teacher-coach team will present their online project to the rest of the group. Coaches and teachers will gain even more knowledge, through the creativity of others, on the uses of technology in the classroom.

These activities all lend themselves to increasing in knowledge about technology, and how to use it as a classroom tool. The innovative element of using student coaches is part of the creative approach to the project. It is not mentioned in the objective because the use of student coaches is not something that is being measured. The use of student coaches is, however, an activity or method that we will use in order to help achieve the measurable objective of increasing knowledge gains.

5. *Activities*

Methodology

A. Contents

a. specific ways each objective you've listed will be accomplished

b. description of project elements, such as sequential events, program staffing, program clients and client selection, timelines

B. Qualities

a. clear explanation of what you're going to do

b. justification—why project will work

6. *Evaluation*

A. Contents

a. evaluation of the result of your project

b. evaluation of how the project has gone and how different activities related to its effectiveness

B. Qualities

a. evaluation tools should be creative.

I assisted on a grant project addressing the problem of elementary-school students' lack of geographical knowledge. Part of the evaluation plan was to determine how much children knew about a certain state in America before an extensive study of the state was begun. Here again, it was a brand of pre- and post-testing, but we gave it a creative twist. Parents were asked to come in to administer an oral pre-test, but they were dressed like a person whose name matched the state (Indiana Jones, Joe Montana, Tennessee Tuxedo, etc.). Not only was this a creative idea, but it brought the parents into the project and allowed them to be creative as well. I recall the two best parents as being Wes Konsin (complete with the cheese hat and Green Bay Packers jersey) and Al Abama (dressed as a Confederate soldier).

7. *Future Funding*

Letting the funder know that you understand the temporary nature of the funding relationship

A. Contents

a. list of different ways you will garner support once funding from current funder runs out

Let's say that you are applying for a grant that will produce an educational CD-ROM as an end product. You tell the funder that your creative idea will live on after the grant through sales of the CD-ROM. This indicates to the funder that your grant will not die once the funding cycle is complete. Or, you may state that your school district will provide necessary training that grant funds will support for the time being. Again, this tells a funder that your grant is not a flash in the pan, and that you are in this for the long haul regardless of the availability of their grant funds.

b. list of ways you will continue to search for more funding from other sources

B. Qualities:

a. forthrightness

b. creativity

c. awareness that current funder may lead you to future sources

8. *Budget*

A grant proposal's budget can be a simple or a confusing document. It depends on the funder. As a general rule, government funders have complicated budget forms and the most extensive budget categories. Don't let that scare you away. It's often good exercise to do detailed research on your planned expenditures—it makes your objectives and activities become that much more clear.

Budgets required by foundation or corporation funders usually ask for much less in terms of a detailed budget because they are not held to the same strict accountability standards as government agencies. These are generalizations, however, with their own set of exceptions. Stick to the following rules when creating a budget and you will have no problem.

Budget Rules

- **Separate personnel costs from non-personnel costs.** This makes your budget page very clear regarding how much funding goes toward salaries, stipends and consultant fees, and how much goes toward hardware, travel, and supplies. A funder can easily determine where most of your needs lie by glancing at the amounts in both of these categories.

* **Make a best guess.** Understand that a budget is your best estimate of what an item or service may cost, based on some research. You can always do the "lazy man's budget" and simply guess what things may cost, but this often fails. Research the cost of items and services, but don't get bogged down in this activity. If part of your budget calls for a laptop computer, don't guess that the one you want will cost around $4,000. Call three or four vendors and ask them for prices on your specific laptop with a 1.3 gigabyte hard drive, 16 megabytes of RAM, a color active matrix screen, and a 28.8 baud internal modem. If the cost is $5,541.33, then get this in writing from the vendor and note on your budget the following information:

  Laptop computer, 1.3 gig HD, 16 mg RAM,
  color active screen, 28.8 int. modem $5550.00

  It is acceptable to round this figure up to the nearest tenth. It is not acceptable to write this amount as $5,600.00 or $6,000.00. The funder has every right to assume that you have researched your budget and are offering them your best estimate (not your best *guess*) of your project's costs. You have every right to assume that some of your guesses may have not been accurate, and that the funder will allow you to move some funds around between budget categories after their permission to do so is obtained.

* **Stay away from generalities.** It is unwise to list a budget category such as Contingency or Miscellaneous, then attach to that category a large amount. This will cause immediate suspicion on the part of the funder and you will lose credibility. On the other hand, there are rare occasions when a budget item fits no other category but Contingency or Miscellaneous. When that is the case, be sure to explain the large amount either by an asterisked reference at the bottom of the budget page or in a budget narrative.

* **List all in-kind contributions.** Every item and service has a value attached to it; many of these are overlooked when budgets are prepared. If your school or school district is committing money, time, or services of any kind to a grant project, then you should note this on your budget as an *in-kind* contribution or shared expense. Most budgets have two separate columns for dollar amounts: Requested and In-Kind. Don't be modest when stating to the funder what you are contributing to the project. Conversely, if you do not have the resources to contribute much (if anything) to the project, don't be embarrassed if your In-Kind column appears rather skimpy, or is entirely nonexistent.

Summary

There you have it—the eight basic elements of a grant proposal. You should be aware that some grant applications (especially reactive grant applications) will not ask for all eight elements. Some may only ask for one or two. This is perfectly normal and, if you think about it, makes sense for reactive grants. Most reactive funders have already identified the problem to be addressed, and they already know how much money they're going to award, which does away with the Needs Assessment and Budget. Many simply don't ask for a Summary/Abstract or Introduction. Several only want to know your Objectives, Activities/Methodology and Evaluation to satisfy their needs. If

this is the case then your work is cut out for you, but you must still remember the characteristics of each proposal element and write them accordingly.

The eight basic elements are showing up more frequently in government grants and foundation/corporation grants. These days it is common to see an application from an agency like the National Science Foundation (NSF) asking for fifteen pages of "project description." If you were to write fifteen pages of rambling descriptive prose, the folks up at NSF would probably disapprove. On the other hand, if you were to break up the fifteen pages into the eight basic proposal elements, the NSF would be given the impression that you know about grant proposals and would probably be a good steward of grant funds. Proactive grants from foundations and corporations are very similar. You may be asked to write a ten-page proposal with no further clarification. Here again your knowledge of the eight basic proposal elements will give you a framework from which to write, and will instill credibility and confidence in your funder.

Each of the eight proposal elements also carries with it a certain weight, which will not vary much from grant to grant. This is how I would divide up the pages of a ten-page proposal:

Abstract/Summary	Usually does not count as a page
Introduction	No more than one page
Needs Assessment	No more than one page
Objectives	No more than two pages
Activities/Methodology	No more than three pages
Evaluation	No more than one and one-half pages
Future Funding	No more than half page
Budget	One page

A Final Word About Proposal Submission

A grant proposal is a professional document. If you want to become even more credible to your funder, you should learn the basic rules of desktop publishing. A great resource for learning about desktop publishing is a small, inexpensive, yet tremendously useful book, *The MAC Is Not a Typewriter* (or *The PC Is Not a Typewriter*, whichever format you use), by Robin Williams (Peachpit Press; Addison, Wesley, Longman).

Chapter 7

Beginnings and Endings

Wow! I Got One!

Congratulations! You've been funded. Now what? Don't worry. The wheels have been set in motion and everything that happens from here on is designed to help you. Funders will not bring you into the grant world, then leave you to fend for yourself. The whole grant process revolves around starting partnerships, and that is exactly what's been awarded to you—a partnership. You must learn how to use the partnership to your advantage and to the advantage of your students.

First, you will receive a telephone call or letter announcing that you have won a grant. Go ahead. Celebrate! But also remember that there are some issues still to iron out before you sign on the dotted line (and, yes, there is a dotted line to sign).

- Make sure that your *submitted* proposal has been accepted, and that the grant you are being awarded is based on the objectives, activities, evaluation, and budget that were outlined in the original proposal.
- If there have been some adjustments made by the funder, then you need to find out about them. If these adjustments cause your proposal to be altered in any way, then further negotiations with the funder may be needed. You must thank the funder for having confidence in your creative approach, but add a reminder that the proposal was carefully thought out and developed.
- If the funder is making changes in funding (perhaps giving you less than what you requested), then you need time to realign your objectives and

activities so that they represent the new budget amounts. The worst case scenario is that your funder will not agree with this request. If that happens, it was not a good match to begin with and you should very graciously bow out of the partnership. Don't be frightened or embarrassed to do this. Have faith in your ideas and another funder will pick them up very soon. It is better to have no partnership than to have a partnership based on a lack of compromise and vision.

Meet the Grant Agreement

Most grants are awarded based on the original proposal. The funder will forward to you a legal-looking document, the "grant agreement." Grant agreements:

- inform the recipients about important points such as how to request monies and maintain appropriate accounting procedure.
- show how to fill out program and financial reports and when to submit them.
- show how to disseminate the project through press releases and articles.
- in some cases, show how to articulate the ownership of copyrights, patents, or articles arising from the project.

Warning bells should be going off about now. Have your school district's attorney or other qualified person review this document before it is signed. If there is a problem with the agreement, call the funder to discuss it. I have found that grant agreements are standard, generic boilerplates that don't necessarily fit each funded project.

Typically, funders are realistic and helpful if the agreement must be altered. If they are not, however, then you are still able to back out of the grant agreement. If your idea is good enough (and obviously it is or it wouldn't have been funded), there is always someone else who will fund it. Don't worry about sullying your reputation by turning down a grant because of a strict agreement. You'll be respected for being patient and waiting to find the right match for your creative ideas. Again, this worst case scenario rarely happens, but be aware that grant agreements are legally-binding documents. If you don't agree with what yours says, don't sign it.

Involve Your Local Funder

The grant agreement will also require you to submit periodical reports on your progress and expenditures. Make these reports very complete and very clear, and get them in on time. Some funders have to make call after call to grant recipients, asking for updates and reports. If yours are timely, accurate, and complete, you will make a lasting impression on your funder. I cannot stress enough the importance of these simple acts of courtesy, gratitude, and sharing. They mean very little to those who receive grant money, but they mean everything to those who give it.

After your grant project is funded, you install computer equipment, or conduct teacher training, or even supervise special classroom activities. Whatever you're doing (that is tied in with the grant) and wherever the geographic location, invite your funder to all events. Many funding organizations allow their program officers to make site visits, so if you think your funder in Baltimore would never come to your grant-supported third-grade opera in San Diego,

think again. Include your funder in everything you do, and give them ownership in your project by providing constant information. Have your kids send thank-you cards or pictures. Please remember that this is a partnership, and treat your funder as an equal partner.

As you near the end of your grant, your funder will be a valuable resource if you have maintained a good partnership. Many program officers are familiar with one another's work and organizations. They speak frequently with one another at conferences, dinners, and over the phone. It is their job to bring in creative projects to their boards so that their philanthropic missions continue to be carried out. If you are a good steward of grant money, and if you are a good partner in a grant relationship, then your program officer will be more than happy to give you helpful advice and ways to leverage additional support with important contacts.

Making Adjustments

Follow your proposal's objectives and activities, but if something isn't working out the way you wish it would, call the funder and see if adjustments can be made. Spend every bit of the money you've been awarded. You've asked for the funds in your budget, so spend them and don't feel guilty about doing it. If you've miscalculated on one of your budget categories and would like to transfer funds from one account to another, discuss this with and get an opinion from your funder. Most times a funder will allow you to shift no more than ten percent of one budget category into another, but with a good enough reason this rule can be bent. The important point is to use the funder's knowledge and expertise to help you throughout your project.

Smart grant recipients make it a habit to contact their funders once every month to give a status report. This way, a crisis situation is averted before it even begins. In the end, the partnership mentality yields successful grant projects and earns the grant recipient a reputation for competence, integrity and adherence to goals.

Oh No! I've Been Rejected!

It's happened to all of us and it will happen again. Having your grant proposal rejected by a funder is certainly no fun, but it does not mean that your creative idea is worthless. I see rejection simply as a mismatch between my idea and the funder I've chosen. In no way do I allow it to diminish the enthusiasm I've had all along for my creative approach. Nor do I allow rejection to stop my forward momentum. If I'm not sure whether or not I'll be funded by an organization (and I'm never absolutely sure), then I always try to line up a few others just in case. Rejection is part of the business, but there are ways that you can make a rejected grant proposal work in your favor.

Nothing to Hide

Most funders allow rejected applicants the opportunity to review the notes and scores of the proposal reviewers. After all, there is nothing to hide. When proposals are read they are given a score. Reviewers are required to write out both positive and negative comments attributed to each one. Then they meet as a group and the scores are combined and averaged so that the best proposals rise to the top. This process is followed by extensive discussion until the reviewers agree on their funding choices. It doesn't always work like this, but you can expect a similar process no matter what type of philanthropic organization you're dealing with. You are eligible to review what others thought about your proposal. All you need to do is ask.

Requesting a review of scores from the funder should be done on a positive note. It does no good to be defensive or to act as if you've been cheated in not getting funded. You may have struck up a congenial relationship with a program officer during the course of promoting and submitting your grant, but the program officer does not make funding decisions. Don't take your frustration out on someone with no control over the process. Instead, thank the organization and the program officer for allowing you to apply for the grant, and request a review of scores so that you can use the constructive criticisms to make your proposal even better.

An organization may invite you to re-submit your proposal once the suggested changes are made. Or, the organization may recommend another funder whose priorities are more of a match with yours. Sometimes the funder will not offer you a review of scores. In that case, smile and go about your business. However, I have never heard of a philanthropic organization that wasn't prepared to offer every bit of advice and service to a rejected grant applicant. Funders are not in the business of being nasty, and I'm sure you will have all of your questions answered.

Looking at the Bright Side

Rejected proposals also result in a test of true leadership and character building. The grant team and outside collaborators all must be told that the funding match did not work out. The way they are told can mean a lot to the future of the project. Resist the temptation to hang your head and throw up your hands in defeat. You have *not* been defeated! Take the rejected grant proposal and rework it, breathe new life into it, and quickly get it to another funder. You've already done all the work by creating, designing, molding, and solidifying your wonderfully creative idea. Don't give up now. Sit down with your team, pull out Funding Target #2, and get that thing in the mail. Maintain the attitude that this project will get off the ground no matter what the odds—that's how strongly you believe in your idea. Whatever you do, don't give up. It's easy to be a good winner, but it's difficult to be a good loser. Show funders your conviction and fortitude, impressive traits by anyone's standards.

Some school districts set up grant programs in which the rate of success is measured by how many grants are applied for each year, and then how many of those are actually funded. If these programs can get half of their grants funded through the saturation approach, then they are happy. In fact, many programs build in perks for the grant writers by paying them a percentage of the grant's bottom line dollar amount. I vehemently disagree with this approach because it goes against the very definition of what constitutes a grant: a creative approach to an existing educational problem. Can one school district really have this many workable creative approaches to all of these problems? Could it have gone through the development and collaboration processes for each of the grants it has submitted? Has the district really taken the time to establish relationships with each of their potential funders? If it has, then I'd like to meet the staff because they have done the impossible.

Product over process is the rule of thumb for grants. Concentrate on developing creative ideas, matching those up with the right funders, and writing professional proposals. When you are rejected, the creative idea does not go away. Move it on to another funder until the right match is found. Rather than flood the market with a bunch of spur-of-the-moment grant ideas that bring in quick money (that doesn't last long) and instant results (that are typically flawed), concentrate instead on one grant idea and try over and over again to get it funded. If your staff, parents, and the community have bought into the idea as a creative and effective approach to an educational problem, then chances are the right funder will buy into it as well. You must have confidence in this approach; it works better than any other. After a time rejection will seem like a minor hurdle rather than the end of the world. It will represent a simple realignment of strategy rather than the destruction and rebuilding of what was a perfectly good idea in the first place.

A Step-by-Step Approach

You now have enough information to write grant proposals of quality and creativity, so what are you waiting for? This is a good place to present the steps book into a simple outline. But remember, one of the best traits you can have is flexibility. Don't feel constrained by my outline or my grant process. In fact, I encourage you to come up with your own.

Always strive for these three elements in everything you do: creativity, simplicity, and clarity.

Step 1—Set Funding Priorities

Meet with your school community to determine what educational problems or issues you will address.

Step 2—Develop Creative Approaches

Engage in continual discussion and brainstorming to develop creative ways to address the agreed-upon problems or issues.

Step 3—Establish a Grant Team

Put the Grant Team in motion with a separation of duties and responsibilities.

Step 4—Identify Grant Opportunities

Match your creative approaches to either reactive or proactive funders.

Step 5—Write Your Proposal

Either complete reactive grant proposals or follow the eight elements of a grant proposal to complete proactive grant proposals.

Step 6—Submit Your Proposal

Prepare for grant acceptance (management plan) or grant rejection (alternate funders).

Step 7—Manage Your Success

Disseminate your project and continually seek additional funding.

Step 8—Repeat the Process

Creativity breeds creativity—build from your ideas and begin more innovative projects.

Bibliography

Brewer, Ernest W. et al. *Finding funding: Grantwriting for the financially challenged educator*. Thousand Oaks, CA: Corwin Press, Inc.

The Chronicle of Philanthropy. P.O. Box 1989, Marion, OH.

Corporate and Foundation Grants. Rockville, MD: Taft Group.

DeAngelis, James, Editor. *The Grantseeker's Handbook of Essential Internet Sites*. Alexandria, VA: Capitol Publications.

Education Grants Alert. Alexandria, VA: Capitol Publications.

Ferguson, Jacqueline. *Grants for schools: How to find and win funds for K–12 programs*. Alexandria, VA: Capitol Publications.

Grantsmanship Book. Los Angeles, CA: Granstmanship Center.

Hall, M.S.. *Getting funded: A complete guide to proposal writing* (3rd ed.). Portland, OR: Continuing Education Publications.

Lefferts, Robert. *Getting a Grant in the 1990s: How to write successful grant proposals*. New York: Simon & Schuster.

National Guide to Funding for Elementary and Secondary Education. New York, NY: The Foundation Center.

Appendices

Project CROAK!
(Creeks, Rivers, Oceans And Kids!)

A proposal submitted to the
National Environmental Education & Training Foundation
Washington, D.C.

Start date: August, 1994
End date: August, 1995
Amount Requested: $41,463.00

Title page should include the project name, to whom it is being written, start and end dates, amount requested, and who's submitting it.

Submitted by:
Dennis M. Norris
Director of Development & Public Relations
Metropolitan School District of Perry Township

5401 S. Shelby Street
Indianapolis, IN 46227
(317)780-4267 / FAX (317)780-4265
dnorris@iquest.net

Project CROAK!
(Creeks, Rivers, Oceans And Kids!)

Abstract

The goal of Project CROAK! is to create collaborative partnerships between elementary students and teachers which serve to blend the study of environmental science and the practice of creative thinking into an interactive curriculum. Beginning in September, 1994, the imaginary Mac the Frog will escape from Douglas MacArthur Elementary School in Indianapolis, Indiana. His travels will take him along the watershed that begins at nearby Buck Creek, traces the White, Wabash, Ohio and Mississippi Rivers, then terminates at the Gulf of Mexico. Along the way, monthly partner schools will be responsible for using IBMs *Linkway* software to develop computer folders about their portion of the waterway. Students will describe special characteristics of their waterways, identify possible sources of pollution and discuss any environmental issues which would concern Mac the Frog as his journey downstream continues. Using creative thinking skills, students will construct theories on how Mac the Frog got from one place to the other, and they will organize their thoughts into creative text. Each month the *Linkway* folders and associated stories will be collected from the partner schools and updated into one larger folder by the Douglas MacArthur staff. By the end of the project each participating school will receive the entire folder of the waterway journey, as well as the cumulative creative text of the partner students. All partners will work together to develop a seamless, creative vehicle for learning more about their environment and associated waterways.

Project CROAK! targets elementary schools that are hard to reach because of their rural or inner-city locations. However, each partner school is located within close proximity to the associated watershed. Participants will be encouraged to incorporate text, graphics and sound into their *Linkway* folders so that each partner school can enhance their learning through the use of advanced technology. In addition, each partner school will utilize some form of word processing software to write the creative portion of the project, and to collaborate with other partner schools. The project will begin in August, with the beginning of the 1994–95 school year. Monthly partner schools have already been established in the following cities: Princeton, Indiana (Oct.); Mt. Vernon, Indiana (Nov.); Paducah, Kentucky (Dec.); West Memphis, Arkansas (Jan.); Vicksburg, Mississippi (Mar.); Baton Rouge, Louisiana (Apr.); New Orleans, Louisiana (May). Douglas MacArthur teachers will spend the summer combining the different elements of the project for dissemination the following the school year. Therefore, funding should span one year, from August, 1994 to August, 1995.

The total cost for the project is $41,463.00. Each of the sixteen partner schools have agreed to furnish computers, software, inservice training and postage costs as in-kind contributions. In addition, Douglas MacArthur Elementary will install a computer network and wiring so that *Writing to Write* software can be utilized by third grade students as the word processing component of Project CROAK! Douglas MacArthur is a special emphasis school, inviting all students who have an interest in environmental and natural science to attend. By using technology to study the environment, the staff plans to develop even more partnerships in order to have a network of like-minded schools across the nation, all benefiting from the integration of a creative environmental science curriculum.

Remember, the Abstract is sometimes the only thing that gets an initial reading in your proposal. If you want to stay in the running make your first paragraph intriguing.

This Abstract is lengthy, but only because the funder asked that certain elements be included. I was given a one-page restriction on this part of the proposal.

An abstract should stand alone as a description of your project. Many times the funder will use bits and pieces of it for press releases. As the applicant you may do the same.

Table of Contents

Include a table of contents if you have more than 10 pages in your proposal, or if you're asked to include it by your funder.

Need for the Project

Project CROAK! will address the problem that elementary students are not adequately exposed to the interdependent relationships that are established between their own behaviors and the state of the environment. There has been little research conducted on the cognitive understanding of young children as it applies to environmental and ecological issues. The reasons for this are: (1) in modern Western society children have few direct experiences with living things or with complete chains of physical systems; and (2) there is a lack of instructional activities that focus on environmental "common denominators" which serve to link children together in collaborative and interdependent ways. Instruction for elementary students must concern itself with the systematic, connecting relationships that exist between the environment and natural resources, the environment and students, and the environment and other topics of study. In his article "Promoting Ecological Awareness in Children," Stewart Cohen writes:

> We must help children acquire proper respect for the environment. First, children need to develop a greater personal awareness of themselves as participants within the context of the environment. We can understand how we affect, and in turn, are affected by our environment if we monitor our own interactions within the near environment.[1]

Project CROAK! is designed to make students aware of environmental issues, to promote respect for the environment, and to realize the importance of their efforts through collaborative relationships with other students.

At the 1990 United Nations conference on education, Harold Hungerford and Trudi Volk of Southern Illinois University introduced a set of variables which they contend shape environmental behavior. The first variable is environmental sensitivity, described as a person's general knowledge of ecology and attitude toward pollution. Most elementary students have a sense of what ecology is and that pollution harms the environment. Project CROAK! will address the second variable, which is ownership. Hungerford and Volk state that once a person develops environmental sensitivity, the next step would be to seek in-depth knowledge about environmental issues and to have a personal investment in the well-being of the environment. Geneticist David Suzuki, host of television's *The Nature of Things*, says that developing environmental awareness in children in grades kindergarten through fourth is the real challenge. "People who live in an urban, human-centered world have the illusion that we know enough to be able to control and dominate nature," he says. "Our challenge is to reconnect children to their natural curiosity."[2] The third variable, that of empowerment, allows each person to feel they can bring about real change in the environment. In this lineal behavioral progression described by Hungerford and Volk, it is the need to cultivate ownership in order to obtain empowerment that Project CROAK! will address.

> The needs assessment presents the problem you are addressing with your creative idea. Do some cursory research so that your funder knows you truly have a grasp on the problem. Your creative solution will seem more relevant if you've shown an understanding of the issues you are about to address.

Finally, Project CROAK! will address the problem that environmental issues are too often associated solely with the science curriculum. During the early elementary school years students are developing lifelong attitudes about science and the environment. The need to integrate environmental issues into every aspect of the curriculum will result in students who are more aware of environmental problems and who are more likely to take on the tasks of ownership and empowerment. Pam Stryker, winner of the 1992 National Presidential Award in elementary education says that "trying to relate the environment to every area of the curriculum is how education will make a difference."[3] Project CROAK! is designed to integrate studies of the environment into the English/grammar/creative writing curriculum of third grade students. Just as environmen-

> Notice in my needs assessment that I'm not only using scholarly research to delineate the problem, but I'm also using some more familiar resources like David Suzuki, and a teacher, Pam Stryker. It's wise to demonstrate that you have a well-rounded perception of the problem so it's seen from many different viewpoints.

---

[1] Cohen, Stewart (1992). Promoting Ecological Awareness in Children. *Childhood Education*, 68(5), 258–260.

[2] Quoted by Estes, Yvonne B (1993). Environmental Education: Bringing Children and Nature Together. *Phi Delta Kappan*, v.74, K1–K12.

[3] Ibid.

tal studies will be accomplished through collaborative and interdependent methods, so too will the creative writing portion of the project. Those students who do not develop positive environmental attitudes of ownership and empowerment, simply because they do not like science, will now have other opportunities to do so through the English curriculum.

Project CROAK! will demonstrate to students that the condition of the environment depends upon like-minded people, working collaboratively, who have the common goal of environmental preservation. This type of interdependent relationship is too often ignored, and the design of the project will show the effectiveness of interdependency and collaboration. It will also address the problem that the topic of environment, as important as it is, is not regularly integrated into other areas of elementary school curriculum. By targeting third grade students, it is the aim of Project CROAK! staff to introduce the concepts of environmental sensitivity, ownership and empowerment at an age when children are forming lifelong attitudes about the world around them.

The needs assessment does just that—it assesses the need for your project and it presents the problem(s).

Objectives and Purpose

The purpose of Project CROAK! is to develop more environmentally-sensitive children so that they will someday become environmentally-conscious adults. This will be done by allowing third grade students from different states the freedom to form collaborative partnerships with each other. By providing curricular vehicles that link each school and cause the participants to be dependent on one another for information, Project CROAK! will stress that true environmental preservation efforts come about in the same interdependent way. Students will come to understand that environmental issues affect everyone, and that solutions to environmental problems must be the work of every citizen.

Project CROAK! is designed to include schools along a watershed system that leads from Buck Creek near Douglas MacArthur Elementary School, to the White, Wabash and Ohio Rivers, into the Mississippi River and out into the Gulf of Mexico. Much of the affected area is impoverished due to either rural or inner-city isolation. The project will, therefore, be conducted in hard-to-reach areas where opportunities for environmental education are limited. All project participants use IBMs *Linkway* software, as well as some type of word-processing software. The relationships established between schools will depend on the mastery of this technology and the student's use of his or her creative thinking skills.

Take a paragraph or two to set up your objectives. I've gone back to my initial abstract language here to reiterate what the project is all about. This helps the reader understand why the objectives focus on certain topics, and why I think it is important that students show measured gains in those topics.

There are three objectives to Project CROAK!:

Objective 1. At the conclusion of Project CROAK!, third grade participants will demonstrate an overall pre- and post-test knowledge gain of 25% regarding waterborne pollutants and their effects on wildlife. The same increase will be demonstrated regarding waterway interdependency and the importance of unpolluted creeks, rivers and oceans.

An objective tells who [*third graders*] is going to do what [*show an increase in knowledge*], when [*at the conclusion of the project*], and how it will be measured [*with and pre- and post-test*].

Objective 2. Through a monthly teacher-conducted survey at each partner school, Project CROAK! will show an increase in participant understanding and appreciation for collaborative relationships based on environmental issues.

Objective 3. In comparing the previous year's third grade class, each Project CROAK! teacher will analyze the degree of competency obtained by students with manipulative computer software, and then record his/her thoughts about the comparison in an informal report.

Objectives don't have to be long and complicated to be effective.

Each objective will be measured and evaluated on both a local scale (by each participating school) and a national scale (by the Douglas MacArthur staff). The project will show that participating students are being exposed to environmental empowerment by increasing their environmental knowledge. It will also show how collaborative relationships based on common goals can be productive and successful. Finally, the project will demonstrate that competency with technology is a legitimate and effective tool for children to use within a variety of different topics.

Think of the methodology section as the nuts and bolts of your project. I lay out exactly what will happen during the funding period. This is my blueprint. These activities are the means to my ends, which are my measurable objectives.

Methodology

During September, 1994, a group of tadpoles will be removed from Buck Creek near Douglas MacArthur Elementary in Indianapolis, Indiana. Over the course of one month, as the tadpoles develop into frogs, a fictitious event will occur. Once of the frogs, Mac, will escape from the pond and start a waterway adventure beginning at the creek and terminating at the Gulf of Mexico. Third grade students at Douglas MacArthur will begin a search for the frog with the understanding that amphibious animals do not stray far from water. Therefore, the search will be limited to the associated watershed and will involve partner schools located along the watershed.

Also during September, 1994, schools involved in the project will begin third grade instruction in IBMs *Linkway* manipulative software. *Linkway* allows students to create a stack of "cards" so that a progressive series of information is presented to the viewer. Text, sound and graphics can be added to each card as the user desires. A cumulative set of informational *Linkway* cards is called a "folder." Students will also begin instruction in a simple word processing program. Keyboarding and text manipulation, along with essential spelling, grammar and sentence structure will make up the curriculum. Students will be asked at some time during the school year to produce a creative story about Mac the Frog. They will need to be proficient with the technology in order to adhere to the project's time schedule.

Notice that I do not assume the funder knows about *Linkway.* It is good practice to write as if your reader knows a little about your topic and your profession, but probably not much. In other words, the reader can figure out what the word "curriculum" means, but he or she may not know what's meant by "metacognitive learning." Of course, avoid jargon.

In October the collaborative part of the project begins. Douglas MacArthur third grade students will produce an introductory *Linkway* folder which explains to other partner schools that Mac the Frog has escaped. The folder will feature digitized images of Mac in a mugshot array and describe his home environment of Buck Creek, including sources of water pollution and other environmental hazards. Students will explain that they are tracing Mac's probable route of travel along interconnecting waterways. Douglas MacArthur students will also enclose the first chapter of a creative story about the Mac the Frog that highlights his life until the time of his escape.

The first school district to receive the introductory information is located in Princeton, Indiana, along the White River. They will be asked to provide information on their own *Linkway* folder about their portion of the watershed, its potential sources of pollution, and any other environmental facts pertinent to the project. Princeton students will also be asked to use word processing software to amend the creative story about Mac the Frog. It is their responsibility to determine how Mac got from Douglas MacArthur to Princeton (i.e. floated on a stick, hopped onto a speedboat, sneaked into the pocket of a small boy, etc.). Princeton's creative story and *Linkway* folder will be sent on a 3.5" floppy disk, via U.S. Mail, back to Douglas MacArthur. Project CROAK! staff and students will then add Princeton's *Linkway* information onto the introductory disk, and include Princeton's creative writing as Chapter Two of the introductory story. Other participating schools will carry out the same amending activities as the project moves downstream. Introductory information about the watershed and the creative story will become more and more complete as the project "leapfrogs" its way toward the Gulf of Mexico.

You can see how detailed I'm getting here, but the activities with this project could easily become misunderstood if I didn't spell things out completely and clearly.

At this point I'm finished describing the project, so with the rest of the methodology I'll describe the leftover items, like the evaluation plan and the CD-ROM we'll plan to produce.

Two weeks before each school begins Project CROAK! activities, teachers will be contacted by project staff and asked to administer a pre- and post-test to their students. The tests will ultimately be used, in a summative and comparative manner, to measure student familiarity with sources of water pollution in the area; species of wildlife that may be affected by water pollution; how waterways are interdependent of each other; and the importance of maintaining unpolluted creeks, rivers and oceans. Teachers of participating schools will also be asked to conduct a survey regarding attitudes about student-to-student collaboration and how important it is for preserving the environment. This process evaluation will help determine the extent to which project activities played a part in project effectiveness. Finally, in a comparative impact evaluation, each participant school will be asked to identify a nonparticipant class from the previous year which used similar technology. The evaluation will examine student technology competency levels and compare them between student-driven curriculum and technology- or teacher-driven curriculum.

This grant application did not ask specifically for an evaluation section, so I slipped it in. As you will see, the application is a little bit backwards when compared to others. That's OK as long as you know how to write each section.

At the end of Project CROAK!, in May, 1994, Douglas MacArthur staff will work through the summer to produce a cumulative *Linkway* folder of the entire watershed. They will also combine each chapter of the creative writing exercise into one text. Each participant school will be sent a copy of the final products, along with a prepared document that presents the evaluatory findings. The National Environmental Education and Training Foundation will also be sent copies of the final products, as well members of the foundation's board of directors. Nonparticipant schools will be encouraged to purchase the final products at the cost of manufacture only. Each package will have suggestions for replicating the project.

It's important to mention future funding. It shows that the staff is willing to keep the ball rolling after the grant goes away.

Project CROAK! will be formally presented at the annual Indiana Computer Educator's Conference in October, 1995; the Indiana Department of Education's Connecting the Future Conference in November, 1995; and the Perry Township Tech-Know Fair in the Spring of 1995. All of the conferences are held in Indianapolis, Indiana. The current plan is to present the project at the National Education Computing Conference in the Summer of 1995, but the staff will remain alert to national conferences with a more environmental theme. The *Linkway* folder and creative text, along with instructions and suggestions for replication, will be available to any person or organization through Douglas MacArthur or the NEETF. Finally, during the summer of 1995 Douglas MacArthur staff will attempt to publish articles regarding the project and its outcome in appropriate periodicals or journals.

Show your funder that you're going to get the word out—you're going to disseminate. Dissemination will bring in more interest and more money.

Project CROAK! Time Chart

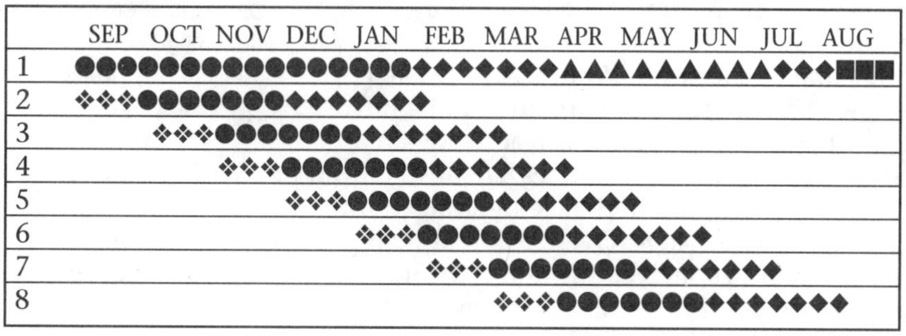

	SEP OCT NOV DEC JAN FEB MAR APR MAY JUN JUL AUG
1	●●●●●●●●●●●●●●●●◆◆◆◆◆◆◆▲▲▲▲▲▲▲▲▲▲◆◆◆■■■
2	❖❖❖●●●●●●●◆◆◆◆◆◆◆
3	❖❖❖●●●●●●●◆◆◆◆◆◆◆
4	❖❖❖●●●●●●●◆◆◆◆◆◆◆
5	❖❖❖●●●●●●●◆◆◆◆◆◆◆
6	❖❖❖●●●●●●●◆◆◆◆◆◆◆
7	❖❖❖●●●●●●●◆◆◆◆◆◆◆
8	❖❖❖●●●●●●●◆◆◆◆◆◆◆

❖ Planning
● Implementation
◆ Evaluation
▲ Supervision
■ Final Product

1 Metropolitan School District of Perry Township
Douglas MacArthur Elementary
Indianapolis, Indiana

2 North Gibson School Corporation
Brumfield Elementary
Princeton, Indiana

3 Metropolitan School District of Mt. Vernon
Farmersville Elementary
Hedges Central Elementary
Marrs Elementary
West Elementary
Mt. Vernon, Indiana

4 Paducah Independent School District
Clark Elementary
Cooper Whiteside Elementary
McNabb Elementary
Morgan Elementary
Paducah, Kentucky

5 West Memphis School District
Jackson Elementary
West Memphis, Arkansas

6 Vicksburg Warren School District
Bowmar Elementary
Beechwood Elementary
Bovina Elementary
Culkin Elementary
Grove Street Elementary
Hall's Ferry Elementary
Jett Elementary
Redwood Elementary
South Park Elementary
Warrenton Elementary
Vicksburg, Mississippi

7 East Baton Rouge Parish Schools
Green Briar Elementary
Baton Rouge, Louisiana

8 Jefferson Parish Public School System
Jefferson Elementary
Jefferson, Louisiana

Not only does a timeline help the reader understand the linear characteristics of the project, but it also shows what fabulous participation we had during the pilot year. It's good to add these visual elements to a proposal, but do so very sparingly and make sure they are understandable.

Four parts of the proposal were omitted here: those that were administrative in nature: Selection of Staff, Training the Staff, Selecting Participants, and Rationale.

Benefits to Environmental Education

Project CROAK! directly benefits environmental education in three ways. First of all, environmental awareness should not be represented as sporadic activity by pockets of concerned citizens—it is more a crucial and constant state of mind that must become an automatic reflex to every citizen. To reach this state of mind requires environmental sensitivity, introduced at as young an age as possible. Once young children grasp the importance of environmental issues, it is up to families and schools to emphasize environmental ownership and empowerment for change. As Barry Lopez notes in his book *The Rediscovery of North America,* children today must be constantly reminded of their affiliation between their actions and the state of the environment:

> We need to sojourn in [the land] again, to discover the lineaments of cooperation with it. We need to discover the difference between the kind of independence that is a desire to be responsible to no one but the self—the independence of the adolescent—and the independence that means the assumption of responsibility in society, the independence of people who no longer need to be supervised.[4]

Nurturing these developmental phases to produce environmentally aware children is a task more easily accomplished through collaboration with others of similar goals. Project CROAK! provides the impetus for collaborative relationships, requiring interdependent participant activities so that the act of collaboration is even more pronounced. Certainly individual efforts or small-scale programs to preserve the environment are noble and necessary undertakings. Project CROAK!, on the other hand, demonstrates that *real* change can only come about by opening up all lines of communication and making available all forms of information to everyone involved. As the environment is an abundance of natural systems, relational chains and lineal progressions, so too must be the methods for its preservation.

Here I explain in a mini-essay what I think are the benefits of my project to environmental education. This part of the proposal is my last chance to convince the reader of the worth of my project. This is my closing argument.

Secondly, Project CROAK! benefits environmental education by suggesting integration of the environment as a subject into all topics of the classroom. By introducing environmental science into creative writing exercises, the project will demonstrate how naturally the two curricula can be linked. The flexibility of the environment as a thematic topic is readily apparent in such other areas as mathematics, reading, language studies, chemistry, even home economics and industrial arts. Environmental awareness should become a byproduct of the educational process just as much as the general increase of knowledge. Overt acts that help preserve the environment should become as natural to humans as sleeping, eating and breathing. Native American cultures equate the health of the environment with life itself. As soon as children begin school they should be taught the same theories, and Project CROAK! helps demonstrate how easily environmental awareness can be integrated into the myriad curricular areas.

Finally, by using computer technologies as a tool to enhance creativity, Project CROAK! benefits environmental education by promoting student-directed learning. It is one thing for students to view films or study texts about the Wabash River or the Mississippi River Delta. Taking the same students to a riverside, allowing them to use all their senses, persuading them to seek out flora and fauna, encouraging investigation of pollution or harmful substances—these are the activities of real learning, of ownership and empowerment. It will be these emotions and experiences that are conveyed through manipulative computer software. Using technology as medium for learning and communicating, students are given a "clean slate" on which they will relate their own agendas and ideas. By allowing students to be creative and imaginative with their environment, the *subject* of environment becomes less an area of pure science and more an area of universal interest. Likewise, using technology as the vehicle for environmental learning makes the *subject* of computers less an experience with an intimidating machine and more an experience for mirroring the mind's eye.

Know your funder's interests. Write for them only and expect them to be excited about what you are saying. As you see, I had to be strong on this part of the proposal because, after all, environmental education is what the NEETF is all about.

[4] Lopez, Barry (1990). *The rediscovery of North America.* Lexington, KY: University of Kentucky Press, p. 49.

Description of Staff and Organization

The Metropolitan School District of Perry Township is among the ten largest school districts in Indiana, with nine elementary schools, the state's two largest middle schools, two high schools, and an overall student population of 12,000. In 1981 the district began a desegregation program, and Perry Township now has a 14 percent minority representation. The district has been the recipient of numerous grants from federal, state, foundation and corporate funders. Schools that receive grants assign a project coordinator, and a district administrator serves as project director. All disbursements are made through the district's business manager under normal Indiana State Board of Accounts guidelines.

Douglas MacArthur Elementary is a "special emphasis" school within the MSD of Perry Township. As an enhancement to the current academic program, the school concentrates on nature and the environment as a platform for teaching students the principles of scientific investigation, problem-solving techniques, and personal responsibility. The goal of Douglas MacArthur's staff, administration and parent groups is to create a learning atmosphere in which students can apply environmental knowledge to make a positive difference in tomorrow's world. Since 1988, Douglas MacArthur has been the annual recipient of the Performance-Based Accreditation Award, which has brought the school over $35,000 in grant funds. During the 1991–92 school year, Douglas MacArthur was designated a Four Star School, and the following year it was the recipient of the Conservation Education Award. Last year, in recognition of the school's promotion of environmental issues, Douglas MacArthur was presented with the Clean Air Award by the State of Indiana.

The project coordinators of Project CROAK! will be the five third grade teachers of Douglas MacArthur Elementary. Marilyn Dial, who has over thirty years teaching experience, serves on the Perry Township Technology Advisory Team and the MacArthur Technology Committee. Ms. Dial is the supervising teacher for both student and cadet teachers, and she heads up the Higher-Level Thinking Team within the school. Beverly Morgan, who has accumulated twenty-eight years of teaching experience, serves on the Math, Reading and English Adoption Committee. Along with Ms. Dial, Ms. Morgan supervises many of the student and cadet teachers and she is also a member of the Higher-Level Thinking Team. Karen Barrett has taught for fifteen years and serves on the design team for the Natural and Environmental Science Focus Committee. Besides chairing the Science Adoption Committee, Ms. Barrett is the Gifted and Talented Coordinator and Peer Facilitator for the school. Joan Schmidt is also one of the project coordinators, and was voted one of the Outstanding Young Women of America in 1986. Ms. Schmidt began her teaching career eleven years ago, after graduating Magna Cum Laude from Indiana University. Beside being a member of the school's Science Committee, Ms. Schmidt stays active in the local chapter of Epsilon Sigma Alpha. Finally, Melanie Payne is also a member of the design team for the Natural and Environmental Science Focus Committee and has eight years teaching experience. Ms. Payne is also part of the Health Adoption Committee, and she chairs the committee to select Mentor Teachers for first year elementary school teachers.

Keep in mind that this application is a little bit backward—the introduction is in the back. No problem, I've still given them introductory information that is relevant to the grant and the acceptance of funds. I started with the district and explained to the funder how things work around here, then I've focused on the school itself. MacArthur has won many awards, but only these few are relevant to the grant for which I am applying. The funder now has a sense that the environment plays a special role in this school, and the staff is dedicated to a curriculum that enhances the mission of environmental education.

Here I provide more detail with a brief description of each of the project coordinators. I show that they are talented and dedicated educators. After reading this paragraph there should be no doubt in the funder's mind that the money will be used as proposed by an experienced group of coordinators and evaluators. I've mentioned activities of each teacher that are relevant to the project and its management. I've tried to show that they are involved and active. The funder can assume that if a problem occurs with the grant it will be handled quickly and professionally.

8

Budget

Personnel

Staff development/training stipends	$1,000.00
Substitutes—$45/day for 10 teachers at 3 days	$1,350.00

Non-Personnel

Subsistence/travel	$500.00
Hardware/software	
Computers—10 IBM PS30s @ $1,966.00/each	$19,660.00
IBM Writing to Write network software	$5,278.00
IBM Kit-B for *Writing to Write* $385/class @ 5 classes	$1,925.00
Materials/supplies	
Postage	$200.00
Supplies	$1,000.00
Printing	$1,500.00
Long distance calls	$800.00
Dissemination activities	
Presentations at 2 Indiana conferences	$2,000.00
Presentation at 1 national conference	$1,000.00
Published articles and materials	$500.00
Indirect costs @10%	$3,750.00
Total Project Cost	$41,463.00

Budget Narrative

Personnel costs include three days of training at $500.00 per software program (*Linkway* and *Writing to Write*). Douglas MacArthur teachers are currently competent in *Linkway*, but will need additional training for the manipulation of sound and graphics. Subsistence/travel expenses under this heading would be for trainees from Princeton and Mt. Vernon, Indiana. Under the hardware/software heading, the costs indicate the introduction of two computers into each of the five third grade classes. Douglas MacArthur students will be responsible for integrating each partner school's folders, graphics, sounds and text into one, and they will need computers capable of performing these tasks. Materials/supplies will cover the costs of mailing disks and text back and forth to partner schools. It also includes the price for printing final versions of the text guide. Long distance calls allow for open communication between schools. Dissemination activities include fees and expenses for presentations at two pre-determined local conferences and one national conference. Other dissemination activities would include processing evaluations of the project, then publishing and presenting the findings.

I try to separate personnel from non-personnel costs, but if the funder doesn't want you to, or if they have their own form, then do it their way. Remember that a budget is your best guess of how much things are going to cost. Always show any in-kind contributions or shared expenses, and always use a budget narrative unless instructed otherwise by the funder.

Tips for Grant Proposal Writing

Abstract / Summary

- Always write as if you are sure you will be funded. Say: This project will train teachers. Do not say: This project, if funded, would train teachers.
- Break your abstract into three main ideas:
    1. Conceptualization of the project
    2. Overview of objectives and activities
    3. Timeline and total amount requested
- If you have writer's block, bring in a stranger and record yourself telling her about the project within five minutes. Replay the tape as a starting point for your writing.
- Use short, crisp sentences with no jargon. Be very clear. Don't use flowery language—stay focused and professional.

Introduction

- Start by describing your school district, or whatever constitutes the "bigger picture." Give a demographic profile and boilerplate information.
- Whittle your way down to the school or classroom, describing staff, students, parents, or community.
- Make your introductions relevant. Investigate awards you have won that would apply to your grant idea, as well as teachers who have special knowledge or talents that apply directly to the grant.
- Make this section interesting by throwing in an inspirational quote from a principal, teacher, parent or, better yet, a student.

Needs Assessment

- Present the problem in broad terms, then hone Problem Statement and specify how it affects your state, district, school and classroom.
- Do cursory research to find some charts/graphs, quotations, studies. Don't overdo this—simply show the funder that you have an awareness of the problem from a variety of perspectives.
- Don't paint a picture of doom. By the same token, don't try to convince the funder that your project will wipe out the problem. Your project should be a creative approach to an existing educational problem or issue—no more, no less.

Objectives

- Objectives are simply outcomes—they are the things that are left over when all is said and done. They may represent learning gains, or a shift in attitudes, a CD-ROM, a log cabin, or a scientific discovery.
- Write them with the understanding that they will help you judge how well you did, or didn't do with your project.
- Research other similar grant projects if you can to see how they did their objectives. This is the value of grants—you, and everyone else before you, help to set up data that can be reviewed and altered as new ideas are attempted. Use the past to help you with the future. Ask funders if they know of projects similar to yours and, if they do, ask how to go about getting copies of those proposals so you can compare objectives.
- Remember to write objectives like everything else in a grant proposal. That is, use positive and confident language: the students will keep journals to show, on a weekly basis, that they understand the aerodynamic concepts presented to them and can relate those concepts through story problems.

Methodology / Activities

- These are the nuts and bolts of your project—the way in which everything will play out. Write activities so that they flow naturally into the objectives. Break up your writing into segments of related activities so that the reader doesn't get bogged down and confused.
- Avoid saying, "Jim Smith will do this and this, and then Mary Doe with do that and that." Instead, refer to project coordinators as "the staff" and other volunteers as "the Parent Committee" or "the Implementation Committee."
- This section is the blueprint for your project, so make it very readable and understandable. If you are abducted by aliens, we should have no problem taking this over for you.
- Be creative with timelines, task charts, job descriptions. The easier you can make the reader understand your project, the better.

Evaluation

- Here is your chance to shine with creativity. The evaluation section tells your funder that you're able to come down from cloud nine with your great idea for awhile and establish some measurable benchmarks. Let's face it, evaluation of any kind is a rather dry topic. Spruce it up with innovative methods and you will boost your chances of being funded dramatically.
- Unless you're preparing an in-depth research grant for MIT, stay away from the very scientific methods of evaluation. You know, all those statistics and bell curves and control groups . . . Yuck! Keep it simple, and keep your language simple. Figure out a way to determine whether or not you reached your objectives, and don't be afraid to tell your funder if you fell a little short of the mark.

Future Funding

* Always tell your funder that this project is so important to you that you will seek additional funds to keep it going. Don't make any promises, just write out that you have a plan (school district will take over funding, a product will be sold, another grant is coming in).
* Here again, use language that is positive and confident: our plan is to approach the Department of Education for additional funds in the fall and, once those are received, leverage even more funds from the ABC Foundation as we have been directed to do by their program officer.
* Usually there is no "The End" part of a grant proposal, so if you want to briefly summarize your project before jumping into the budget, now is the time to do it. I often end with a sentence or two at the end of this section that reminds the funder of how dedicated I am to the project and how much I believe it will address the particular problem.

Budget

* Fill in the blanks if you're provided a budget form. If not, feel free to use the examples from this book. However, if your budget has some strange item that breaks the mold (for instance, if you're buying a pack of llamas for scientific research), then make sure the budget reflects what you're doing. I've seen many examples of budgets, but I never get locked into them. Stay flexible and prepare a budget that reflects your costs.
* Write out a brief budget narrative unless you're told otherwise. Make it very concise and to the point.
* Keep in mind that a budget is your best guest, and if you've misjudged the cost of something the funder will probably work things out with you. That doesn't mean you can be sloppy here, either. Just do the best you can and lay down a figure that represents what you want to do.
* If you suspect that the grant will cause you to work after school hours and involve extra effort, write some extra funds into your budget. Don't be embarrassed about paying yourself for your time and effort. If a funder refuses to fund stipends for you then they are, in fact, not recognizing you as a professional. I would reconsider their grant if this were to happen.

Appendix C

Funders

Reactive Grant Opportunities

American Chemical Society

The American Chemical Society has a wonderful program called Parents and Children for Terrific Science. Grants are awarded to support hands-on science projects that involve children and their parents. Grants are usually around $1,200, and the funder gives preference to applications that provide matching funds. Deadline each year is March 31, and any nonprofit institution or school is eligible.

Contact: Ann Benhow, Pre-High School Science Office, American Chemical Society, 1155 16th Street NW, Washington, DC 20036, (202) 452-2113.

American Heroes in Education Award

Reader's Digest sponsors this grant opportunity each November to recognize teachers and principals who are making a difference in the lives of their students. Elementary and secondary teachers/principals are eligible as individuals or as teams of up to six individuals. Awards are $5,000 for the teacher, principal or team plus an additional $10,000 for the winning school.

Contact: Mary Terry, Reader's Digest American Heroes in Education Award, Pleasantville, NY 10572, (914) 238-1000.

Anheuser-Busch—A Pledge and a Promise Environmental Awards

These grants are sponsored by the Anheuser-Busch Theme Parks, and they honor school groups that develop innovative environmental education projects. Grants are tiered from $20,000 down to $2,500, and winners get to go to one of the theme parks to receive the award. Deadline is usually in January.

Contact: A Pledge and A Promise Environmental Awards, Sea World Education Department, Sea World, 7007 Sea World Drive, Orlando, FL 32821, (407) 363-2389.

Barbara Bush Foundation for Family Literacy

This is a wonderful organization and very receptive to creative ideas. Barbara Bush grants support projects that address the problems associated with the intergenerational cycle of illiteracy. Projects should seek to establish literacy as a value in every family through community planning, training and professional development. Any nonprofit organization or school in the United States is eligible. Deadline is usually in August each year. The foundation usually releases $500,000 in funds for 15–25 grants.

Contact: Barbara Bush Foundation for Family Literacy, 1002 Wisconsin Avenue NW, Washington, DC 20007, (202) 338-2006.

Budget Rent A Car Leadership Development Grant

Budget recognizes the importance of training women as sports leaders, coaches, officials and administrators of female sports programs. Their national grant program has annual deadlines of June 15 and October 31. Eligible are public and private schools, sports organizations that offer female sports, or any individual interested in advancing herself as a professional in this area. Funding amounts vary each year.

Contact: Budget Rent A Car Leadership Development Grants, Women's Sports Foundation, Coaches Advisory Roundtable, 342 Madison Avenue, Suite 728, New York, NY 10173, (800) 227-3988.

Chemical Manufacturers Association Mini-Grants Program

This organization funds grants that use high school chemistry classes and students to improve elementary school science education. The deadline is in December, and $500 grants are awarded for supplies, substitute teachers and transportation.

Contact: Patricia Sokoloff, Manager, Education Services, Minigrant Application, Chemical Manufacturers Association, 1300 Wilson Blvd., Arlington, VA 22209, (703) 741-5825.

Christa McAuliffe Awards

These grants are given by the National Council for the Studies Studies, and they are awarded to social studies teachers who submit proposals outlining a unique ambition. Applicants must be members of the National Council for the Social Studies. Deadline is April 1 of every odd-numbered year. Grants are typically $1,000.

Contact: National Council for the Social Studies, 3501 Newark Street NW, Washington, DC 20016, (202) 966-7840.

Cisco Systems' Virtual Schoolhouse Grants

These grants provide schools with equipment to connect to the Internet. The annual deadline is usually in March, and 50 grants are given of $10,000 worth of hardware. Both elementary and secondary schools are eligible. This grant opportunity gets bigger every year, so it's worth it to call for guidelines.

Contact: Cisco Systems Inc., Virtual Schoolhouse Grants, P.O. Box 5105, Belmont, CA 94002-5105, (408) 526-4226.

C-SPAN Equipment-for-Education Grant

C-SPAN in the Classroom gives video equipment to teachers who develop creative programs that use C-SPAN in the classroom. Deadline is March 14 each year. This is a good way to bring in televisions and VCRs to the classroom.

Contact: C-SPAN in the Classroom, Equipment-for-Education Grant Program, 400 North Capitol Street NW, Suite 650, Washington, DC 20001, (202) 626-4858.

GTE Foundation—GIFT Program

This is one of the better reactive grant opportunities. The GIFT Program (Growth Initiatives for Teachers) supports secondary math and science teachers who team up to design creative projects for their students. Deadline is usually in January, and GTE chooses 60 teams nationwide and gives them $12,000 grants.

Contact: Maureen Gorman, Vice President, GTE Foundation, 1 Stamford Forum, Stamford, CT 06904, (203) 965-3620.

Hilda Maehling Grants Program

The National Foundation for the Improvement of Education sponsors the Hilda Maheling grants, which support innovative teacher projects designed to increase teacher participation in the National Education Association. Project may address professional development issues, the enhancement of teaching skills, or the development of professional tools and techniques. Teachers who belong to the NEA are eligible. Deadline for the grant is usually in February each year, and there are one or two awards given at $4,000 each.

Contact: Donna C. Rhodes, Executive Director, National Foundation for the Improvement of Education, 1201 16th Street NW, Washington, DC 20036, (202) 822-7840.

Hitachi Foundation Grants

The Hitachi Foundation issues these grants each year for creative projects that promote an understanding of diversity and global issues across disciplines, foster links between community service and education, and increase work-force development. Public and private schools are eligible, and applicants must submit pre-proposals before February 1 and October 1. The foundation will notify you shortly after these dates to request a full proposal. Grants range from $1,500 to $250,000.

Contact: Hitachi Foundation, 1509 22nd Street NW, Washington, DC 20037, (202) 457-0588.

Implementation and Development Projects for Women and Girls

The National Science Foundation gives grants each year for projects that build on existing research about gender and math, science and engineering in an effort to promote change in the methods by which women and girls are taught technical subjects. Preliminary proposals are due each October, and invited formal proposals are due by May. Grants are usually in the $100,000 range.

Contact: Implementation and Development Projects for Women and Girls, Division of Human Resource Development, Directorate for Education and Human Resources, National Science Foundation, 4201 Wilson Blvd., Arlington, VA 22230, (703) 306-1637.

Instructional Materials Development

The National Science Foundation is another philanthropic giant for schools. This program supports projects that develop strategies and materials to improve instruction in science, mathematics, and technology. Although the grants are for grades K–12, the projects should seek collaborative relationships between secondary schools and colleges. School districts are eligible, and deadlines for the program are May 15 and November 15 each year. The amount of funding varies with federal legislation and appropriation.

Contact: Materials Development, Research and Informal Science Education, National Science Foundation, 1800 G Street NW, Washington, DC 20550, (202) 357-7066.

Japanese Studies Grants

These grants are awarded by the Northeast Asia Council and Association for Asian Studies, along with the Japan-United States Friendship Commission. Teachers of Japanese are eligible for these grants, which allow attendance at seminars, travel, and research in Japanese studies. Projects should focus on individual research, improving the quality of teaching, and the integration of Japanese into the major academic disciplines. Deadlines are March 1 and November 1 each year. Grants range from $1,000 to $5,000, depending upon the nature and duration of the project.

Contact: Northeast Asia Council of the Association for Asian Studies, University of Michigan, One Lane Hall, Ann Arbor, MI 48109-1290, (313) 665-2490.

Just Do It Teachers' Grants

The National Foundation for the Improvement of Education and NIKE Inc. support this dropout prevention program. Grants are used to fund projects that promote and encourage academic success with at-risk students. Any teacher in the United States is eligible, at any K–12 grade level. Deadline is usually in February, and grants can be awarded between $5,000 and $25,000.

Contact: National Foundation for the Improvement of Education, Dropout Prevention Program, 1201 16th Street NW, Washington, DC 20036, (202) 822-7840.

NASA's Educational Workshops for Math, Science and Technology

The National Aeronautics and Space Administration and the National Science Teachers Association support this grant opportunity, which comes due each year on February 15. The grant allows over 200 K–12 teachers to spend two weeks at a regional NASA research center to learn the process of integrating aerospace science into the curriculum. Any math, science, or technology teacher is eligible, as is any elementary school teacher. The grant covers the cost of the workshop, transportation, and housing.

Contact: NEWMAST/NEWEST Workshops, National Science Teachers Association, 5112 Berwyn Road, Third Floor, College Park, MD 20740, (301) 474-0487.

National Endowment for the Arts Design Arts Education Grants

These grants are for public and private schools, school districts, and nonprofit organizations. They support creative projects that produce design arts education materials, teacher training and conference attendance. The main focus of these projects should be on students from preschool through high school. Deadlines are usually in June and December each year, but check with the Endowment to be sure. Grants range from $5,000 to $25,000.

Contact: Design Arts, National Endowment for the Arts, 1100 Pennsylvania Avenue NW, Room 625, Washington, DC 20506, (202) 682-5437.

National Endowment for the Humanities Collaborative Projects

One of the many NEH grant programs that come around each year for schools, this program asks applicants to design collaborative projects between schools and higher education, libraries or museums. In what usually amounts to a multi-year partnership between the partners, projects should focus on humanities topics. This is a national competition with deadlines on March 15 and December 15 each year. Pre-proposals and project reviews with an NEH program officer are highly recommended. Grants are usually $200,000 each for two years.

Contact: Division of Research Programs, National Endowment for the Humanities, 1100 Pennsylvania Avenue NW, Room 302, Washington, DC 20506, (202) 606-8377.

Newman's Own Inc.

The Newman's Own organization gives grants each September for K–12 projects that help disadvantaged children and youths. The grant dollars are dependent upon the company's profit each year, but grants average between $500 and $25,000.

Contact: Newman's Own Inc., 246 Post Road East, Westport, CT 06880, (203) 222-0136.

Technology, Media and Materials for Individuals With Disabilities

These federal grant come from the Education Department, and these are for innovative designs that help students with disabilities adapt to technology. They also award grants that promote state-of-the-art instructional environments both in and out of school. Deadline is usually is April each year, and grants average $200,000.

Contact: Robin Murphy, Education Department, 600 Independence Avenue SW, Room 4617, Switzer Building, Washington, DC 20202-2734, (202) 205-9884.

Toyota's Investment in Mathematics Excellence

Toyota and the National Council of Teachers of Mathematics sponsor these grants for K–12 math teachers with creative ideas for improving math education. Grants are $10,000 each, and recipients attend a summer seminar sponsored by Toyota. Deadline is usually in December.

Contact: L. Eileen Erickson, National Council for Teachers of Mathematics, 1906 Association Drive, Reston, VA 22091-1593, (703) 620-9840 x102.

Toyota TAPESTRY Grants

Another one of the better reactive grants, Toyota and the National Science Teachers Association team up each year to fund projects that enhance science education for K–12 schools. The deadline varies, but it is usually in January. Several one-year grants of $10,000 are awarded. Projects should be creative, risk-taking and visionary.

Contact: Eric Crossley, National Science Teachers Association, Toyota TAPESTRY, 1840 Wilson Blvd., Arlington, VA 22201-3000, (703) 312-9258.

United States Institute of Peace

These grants are given in October and April each year for projects that support education and professional development regarding international peace. Grants range from $5,000 to $50,000, with an average of $30,000. Any K–12 school is eligible, but the organization encourages projects from secondary schools.

Contact: United States Institute of Peace, 1550 M Street NW, Suite 700, Washington, DC 20005-1708, (202) 429-3845.

Youth Garden Grants Program

The National Gardening Association sponsors these grants that encourage schools and community organizations to teach children about plants and gardening. The annual deadline is in November, and grants come in the form of tools, seeds, plants and garden products. There are typically 300 awards given each year.

Contact: Youth Garden Grants Program, Department PS, National Gardening Association, 180 Flynn Avenue, Burlington, VT 05401, (800) 538-7476.

Proactive Grant Opportunities

Alcoa Foundation

The Alcoa Foundation awards grants that support education, especially as it applies to economics. There are no annual deadlines. Applicants are encouraged to write or call the foundation for grant guidelines. In the past Alcoa's giving priorities have been in mathematics, science and tutoring programs for public schools. They usually give funding preference to applicants near communities in which Alcoa plants or offices are located.

Contact: Alcoa Foundation, 1501 Alcoa Building, Pittsburgh, PA 15219-1850, (412) 553-2348.

American Express Philanthropic Program

The focus of this organization is to provide funding for projects that stimulate employment opportunities for young people, promote education reform and increase geographic literacy. There are no annual guidelines, and applicants are encouraged to write or call the foundation for grant guidelines. Any tax-exempt organization is eligible for the program, but preference is given to applicants from communities in which American Express has a presence.

Contact: Mary Beth Salerno, Vice President, American Express Philanthropic Program, American Express Tower, World Financial Center, New York, NY 10285-4710, (212) 640-5661.

Ameritech Foundation

Support from the Ameritech Foundation is limited to the Great Lakes region, and it focuses on programs that seek to improve K–12 education generally, and K–12 economic programs specifically. Write the program officer with your project idea before applying.

Contact: Michael Kuhlin, Director, Ameritech Foundation, 30 S. Wacker Drive, Chicago, IL 60606.

Borg-Warner Foundation

The Borg-Warner Foundation awards grants in the areas of early childhood education, principal leadership programs and minority student scholarships. The annual deadline is usually March 1. The foundation gives nationally, but organizations from the Chicago area have a better chance at getting funded.

Contact: Ellen Benjamin, Director of Corporate Contributions, Borg-Warner Foundation, 200 S. Michigan Avenue, Chicago, IL 60604, (312) 322-8659.

Bristol-Myers Squibb Foundation

Education, science, medical and cultural projects are the philanthropic interests of this foundation. The deadline for proposal submission is October 1 each year, but call a program officer to discuss your idea long before then. Schools and tax-exempt organizations are eligible to receive funding.

Contact: John Damonti, Manager, Bristol-Myers Squibb Foundation, 345 Park Avenue, New York, NY 10154, (212) 546-4566.

Chevron USA

Like many large US corporations, Chevron has a corporate contributions program that gives grants to schools and nonprofits. Chevron encourages environmental education projects, as well as K–12 mathematics and science programs. There are no annual deadlines, so applicants must call Chevron to receive grant guidelines.

Contact: Linda Van Heertum, Contributions Representative, Corporate Contributions, Chevron USA, P.O. Box 7753, San Francisco, CA 94120, (415) 894-4193.

Clorox Company

The Clorox Company's community programs award grants that improve education, with a special focus on minority students and low-income youths. There are quarterly deadlines throughout the year for these grants. Clorox funding priorities in the past have been in the areas of literacy for minority youth, college preparation and reducing the incidence of at-risk students.

Contact: Carmella Johnson, Contributions Manager, Clorox Company, P.O. Box 24305, Oakland, CA 94623, (415) 271-7747.

Danforth Foundation

Reorganization of schools and professional development for teachers are the two main philanthropic interests of the Danforth Foundation. There are no annual deadlines. Applicants should call a program officer to discuss their project. Any tax-exempt organization is eligible, including schools.

Contact: William Danforth, Chairman, Danforth Foundation, 231 S. Bemiston Avenue, Suite 1080, St. Louis, MO 63105-1903, (314) 862-6200.

The Geraldine R. Dodge Foundation

This foundation gives grants for national programs in secondary education, public issues and the arts. There are quarterly deadlines, so call the foundation to see which deadline applies to you. Tax-exempt organizations and schools are eligible.

Contact: Scott McVay, Executive Director, Geraldine R. Dodge Foundation, 95 Madison Avenue, P.O. Box 1239, Morristown, NJ 07962-1239, (201) 540-8442.

Educational Foundation of America

This particular foundation gives proactive grants for many different programs, including education, environment, peace, nuclear energy use, medicine, and Native American issues. Schools and other nonprofits are eligible, and there is no set annual deadline. Projects should be very innovative in nature.

Contact: Diane Allision, Executive Director, Educational Foundation of America, 35 Church Lane, Westport, CT 06880, (203) 226-6498.

Exxon Education Foundation

Exxon funds creative programs that emphasize mathematics. There are no annual deadlines, and any school or nonprofit is eligible.

Contact: Mathematics Education Program, Exxon Education Foundation, 225 E. John W. Carpenter Freeway, Irving, TX 75062-2298, (214) 444-1104.

Ford Foundation

This very large foundation funds projects that strengthen the teaching profession and provided opportunities for at-risk and disadvantaged youths. Nonprofits are eligible, including schools. There is no annual deadline.

Contact: Office of Communications, Ford Foundation, 320 E. 43rd Street, New York, NY 10017, (212) 573-5169.

W. K. Kellogg Foundation

Kellogg is an enormous foundation with interests in education and projects that address human problems. There are no annual deadlines, and although the foundation funds nationally, the emphasis is on Michigan. Applicants need to write or call the foundation for information on the many programs.

Contact: W.K. Kellogg Foundation, One Michigan Avenue East, Battle Creek, MI 49017-4058, (616) 968-1611.

Kraft General Foods

Kraft has an interest in funding programs designed to increase the capability of the workforce through sound educational practices. Schools may apply, but Kraft has an interest in funding nonprofits run by and for the disabled, women and minorities. There are no annual deadlines.

Contact: Administrative Director, Kraft General Foods Foundation, 250 North Street, White Plains, NY 10625, (914) 335-2500.

John D. and Catherine T. MacArthur Foundation

The MacArthur Foundation supports collaborative grant projects that focus on improving children's reading and mathematics skills. Schools may apply, and the board meets nearly every month to make funding decisions. This organization has many programs, so you should write or call for a description of the whole spectrum.

Contact: James Furman, Executive Vice President, John D. and Catherine T. MacArthur Foundation, 140 S. Dearborn Street, Chicago, IL 60603, (312)726-8000.

Mars Foundation

Mars is another supporter of innovative education projects. The board meets in June and December of each year. Tax-exempt organizations are welcome to apply, as are schools.

Contact: Roger Best, Secretary, Mars Foundation, 6885 Elm Street, McLean, VA 22101-3883, (703) 821-4900.

Mobil Foundation

Mobil's primary philanthropic interests are in education and youth programs. There are no annual deadlines, and any school may apply.

Contact: Mobil Foundation, 3225 Gallows Road, Fairfax, VA 22037-0001, (703)846-3000.

Charles Steward Mott Foundation

The Mott Foundation is interested in bringing schools and communities together to improve the quality of life. They fund collaborative efforts such as workforce projects, mentoring and tutoring. Any nonprofit is eligible for funding, including schools. There are no annual deadlines.

Contact: Pat Edwards, Program Officer, Charles Steward Mott Foundation, 1200 Mott Foundation Blvd., Flint, MI 48502, (313) 238-5651.

National Geographic Society Education Foundation

This foundation sets new guidelines and programs each year, but they generally fund projects that improve the quality and content of geography education for K–12 schools. It is wise to get on their mailing list.

Contact: Patty Unkel, National Geographic Society Education Foundation, 17th and M Streets NW, Suite 580, Washington, DC 20036, (202) 857-7363.

NYNEX Foundation

This is another foundation that is interested in a capable workforce, and it funds projects in schools that recognize excellence and professionalism in education. There are no annual deadlines, so call with your creative ideas.

Contact: NYNEX Foundation, 1113 Westchester Avenue, First Floor, White Plains, NY 10604-3510, (212) 370-7400.

Oscar Mayer Foods Corporation

Each year Oscar Mayer supports programs dealing with education, hunger and nutrition, culture, humanities and the environment. They tend to fund most heavily in areas where Oscar Mayer facilities are located, but call anyway. There are no annual deadlines and schools are eligible for funding.

Contact: Lynette Byrnes, Civic Affairs Administrator, Oscar Mayer Foods Corporation, P.O. Box 7188, Madison, WI 53707, (608) 241-3311.

James C. Penny Foundation

At-risk students and teen pregnancy are the main philanthropic interests of the JC Penny Foundation, but they also support programs in environmental education. Eligible are tax-exempt organizations and schools. There are no annual deadlines.

Contact: James C. Penney Foundation, 1633 Broadway, 39th Floor, New York, NY 11019, (212) 830-7490.

Sears-Roebuck Foundation

Sears supports creative projects in education, especially those that focus on workforce development and at-risk students. Tax-exempt organizations are eligible, including schools, and there are no annual deadlines.

Contact: Program Manager, Sears-Roebuck Foundation, Department 903, BSC 51-02, Sears Tower, Chicago, IL 60608, (312) 875-2500.

Toyota USA Foundation

Toyota USA awards grants that improve schools, encourage educational excellence and prepare students for the workforce. Tax-exempt organizations and schools are eligible, and there are no annual deadlines. Projects may be directed toward students, teachers and/or administrators.

Contact: Foundation Administrator, Toyota USA Foundation, 19001 S. Western Avenue, Torrance, CA 90509, (213) 618-6766.

United States-Japan Foundation

Creative projects that promote cooperation between these two companies are the foundation's emphasis. They have a high incidence of funding K–12 projects that promote language and culture. Tax-exempt organizations are eligible, as are schools. There are no annual deadlines.

Contact: Stephen W. Bosworth, President, United States–Japan Foundation, 145 E. 32nd Street, New York, NY 10016, (212) 481-8753.